TIME OF THE WOLVES

**Center Point
Large Print**

**This Large Print Book carries the
Seal of Approval of N.A.V.H.**

TIME OF THE WOLVES

Western Stories

Marcia Muller

CENTER POINT PUBLISHING
THORNDIKE, MAINE

This Center Point Large Print edition
is published in the year 2007 by arrangement with
Golden West Literary Agency.

The text of this Large Print edition is unabridged. In other
aspects, this book may vary from the original edition. Printed in
Thailand. Set in 16-point Times New Roman type.

ISBN-10: 1-58547-962-4
ISBN-13: 978-1-58547-962-7

Library of Congress Cataloging-in-Publication Data

Muller, Marcia.
    Time of the wolves : western stories / Marcia Muller.--Center Point large print ed.
        p. cm.
    ISBN-13: 978-1-58547-962-7 (lib. bdg. : alk. paper)
    1. Western stories. 2. Large type books. I. Title.

    PS3563.U397T56 2007
    813'.54--dc22

2006036865

TABLE OF CONTENTS

Foreword

In the early 1980s when I was a struggling new writer, my friend (and now husband) Bill Pronzini suggested I write a short story for a Western anthology he was editing. It seemed like a good idea; after all, I'd watched "Gunsmoke" and "Maverick", hadn't I? But the subject matter proved to be a problem, and it wasn't until I read a news item about a man being killed when a giant saguaro cactus fell on him that I could begin. "Sweet Cactus Wine", in which a benign saguaro commits mayhem, was my first Western tale.

Others followed, set in both the old and new West. Three stories feature characters from two mystery series: In "The Sanchez Sacraments" Santa Barbara-based Mexican-American museum director Elena Oliverez becomes involved in a controversy surrounding the donation of a group of pottery religious figures; San Francisco sleuth Sharon McCone investigates in "The Lost Coast", set in a remote and little-known area in California's Humboldt County, and again in "Knives at Midnight", a case whose solution hinges on a point of law that has been on the books since frontier days.

Travels often inspire story ideas. A visit to an ice cave in Montana resulted in my first collaboration with Bill Pronzini, "Cave of Ice". After an initial rocky start, the success of this joint project ultimately led us to work together on numerous short stories, three novels, various anthologies, and one non-fiction book. While I was traveling in Kansas, the story of a close relationship between an Indian woman and a white settler, "Sisters", was suggested to me by a local history buff. My frequent journeys to the coastal area of Mendocino County prompted me to set "Forbidden Things" there. Years later, in the non-series novel POINT DECEPTION, I would create fictional Soledad County—an amalgam of various northern California locales; "The Indian Witch" and "The Cyaniders" are explorations of the history of those places.

As readers and writers know, the film industry often does strange things to the literary properties it purchases, and that was certainly true of the title story of this volume, "Time of the Wolves". The 1988 Western Writers of America Spur-nominated story was used as the central segment of a made-for-TV movie, INTO THE BADLANDS, a trilogy of western horror/fantasy sales, starring Bruce Dern, Helen Hunt, and Mariel Hemingway. While the story itself is a straightforward tale of a woman settler's ordeal on the Kansas prairie, the 1991 film (whose producers proclaim it as being set "somewhere between civilization and the ninth circle of hell") put a confusing supernatural twist on it, and Dern's over-the-top performance as the narrator, a cold-hearted bounty hunter, was less than successful.

A mediocre film notwithstanding, I've enjoyed

delving into the history and the present-day state of the American West. I hope you will enjoy reading these stories as much as I did writing them.

Marcia Muller
Petaluma, California
March 29, 2002

Sweet Cactus Wine

The rain stopped as suddenly as it had begun, the way it always does in the Arizona desert. The torrent had burst from a near-cloudless sky, and now it was clear once more, the land nourished. I stood in the doorway of my house, watching the sun touch the stone wall, the old buckboard, and the twisted arms of the giant saguaro cacti.

The suddenness of these downpours fascinated me, even though I'd lived in the desert for close to forty years, since the day I'd come here as Joe's bride in 1866. They'd been good years, not exactly bountiful, but we'd lived here in quiet comfort. Joe had the instinct that helped him bring the crops—melons, corn, beans—from the parched soil, an instinct he shared with the Papago Indians who were our neighbors. I didn't possess the knack, so now that he was gone I didn't farm. I did share one gift with the Papagos, however—the ability to make sweet cactus wine from the fruit of the saguaro. That wine was my livelihood now—as well as, I must admit, a source of Saturday-night pleasure—and the giant cacti scattered around the ranch were my fortune.

I went inside to the big rough-hewn table where I'd been shelling peas when the downpour started. The bowl sat there half full, and I eyed the peas with distaste. Funny what age will do to you. For years I'd had an overly hearty appetite. Joe used to say: "Don't

11

worry, Katy. I like big women." Lucky for him he did, because I'd carried around enough lard for two such admirers, and I didn't believe in divorce anyway. Joe'd be surprised if he could see me now, though. I was tall, yes, still tall. But thin. I guess you'd call it gaunt. Food didn't interest me any more.

I sat down and finished shelling the peas anyway. It was market day in Arroyo, and Hank Gardner, my neighbor five miles down the road, had taken to stopping in for supper on his way home from town. Hank was widowed, too. Maybe it was his way of courting. I didn't know and didn't care. One man had been enough trouble for me, and, anyway, I intended to live out my days on these parched but familiar acres.

Sure enough, right about suppertime Hank rode up on his old bay. He was a lean man, browned and weathered by the sun like folks get in these parts, and he rode stiffly. I watched him dismount, then went and got the whiskey bottle and poured him a tumblerful. If I knew Hank, he'd had a few drinks in town and would be wanting another. And a glassful sure wouldn't be enough for old Hogsbreath Hank, as he was sometimes called.

He came in and sat at the table like he always did. I stirred the iron pot on the stove and sat down, too. Hank was a man of few words, like my Joe had been. I'd heard tales that his drinking and temper had pushed his wife into an early grave. Sara Gardner had died of pneumonia, though, and no man's temper ever gave that to you.

Tonight Hank seemed different, jumpy. He drummed his fingers on the table and drank his whiskey.

To put him at his ease, I said: "How're things in town?"

"What?"

"Town. How was it?"

"Same as ever."

"You sure?"

"Yeah, I'm sure. Why do you ask?" But he looked kind of furtive.

"No reason," I said. "Nothing changes out here. I don't know why I asked." Then I went to dish up the stew. I set it and some cornbread on the table, poured more whiskey for Hank and a little cactus wine for me. Hank ate steadily and silently. I sort of picked at my food.

After supper I washed up the dishes and joined Hank on the front porch. He still seemed jumpy, but this time I didn't try to find out why. I just sat there beside him, watching the sun spread its redness over the mountains in the distance. When Hank spoke, I'd almost forgotten he was there.

"Kathryn"—he never called me Katy, only Joe used that name—"Kathryn, I've been thinking. It's time the two of us got married."

So that was why he had the jitters. I turned to stare. "What put an idea like that into your head?"

He frowned. "It's natural."

"Natural?"

"Kathryn, we're both alone. It's foolish you living here and me living over there when our ranches sit next to each other. Since Joe went, you haven't farmed the place. We could live at my house, let this one go, and I'd farm the land for you."

Did he want me, or the ranch? I know passion is supposed to die when you're in your sixties, and as far as Hank was concerned mine had, but for form's sake he could at least pretend to some.

"Hank," I said firmly, "I've got no intention of marrying again . . . or of farming this place."

"I said I'd farm it for you."

"If I wanted it farmed, I could hire someone to do it. I wouldn't need to acquire another husband."

"We'd be company for one another."

"We're company now."

"What're you going to do . . . sit here the rest of your days scratching out a living with your cactus wine?"

"That's exactly what I plan to do."

"Kathryn. . . ."

"No."

"But. . . ."

"No. That's all."

Hank's jaw tightened and his eyes narrowed. I was afraid for a minute that I was going to be treated to a display of his legendary temper, but soon he looked placid as ever. He stood, patting my shoulder.

"You think about it," he said. "I'll be back tomorrow, and I want a yes answer."

I'd think about it, all right. As a matter of fact, as he

rode off on the bay, I was thinking it was the strangest marriage proposal I'd ever heard of. And there was no way Hogsbreath was getting any yesses from me.

He rode up again the next evening. I was out gathering cactus fruit. In the springtime, when the desert nights are still cool, the tips of the saguaro branches are covered with waxy white flowers. They're prettiest in the hours around dawn, and by the time the sun hits its peak, they close. When they die, the purple fruit begins to grow, and now, by midsummer, it was splitting open to show its bright red pulp. That pulp was what I turned into wine.

I stood by my pride and joy—a fifty-foot giant that was probably two hundred years old—and watched Hank come toward me. From his easy gait, I knew he was sure I'd changed my mind about his proposal. Probably figured he was irresistible, the old goat. He had a surprise coming.

"Well, Kathryn," he said, stopping and folding his arms across his chest, "I'm here for my answer."

"It's the same as it was last night. No. I don't intend to marry again."

"You're a foolish woman, Kathryn."

"That may be. But at least I'm foolish in my own way."

"What does that mean?"

"If I'm making a mistake, it'll be one I decide on, not one you decide for me."

The planes of his face hardened, and the wrinkles

around his eyes deepened. "We'll see about that." He turned and strode toward the bay.

I was surprised he had backed down so easy, but relieved. At least he was going.

Hank didn't get on the horse, however. He fumbled at his saddle scabbard and drew his shotgun. I set down the basket of cactus fruit. Surely he didn't intend to shoot me!

He turned toward me. I got ready to run, but he kept going, past me. I whirled, watching. Hank went up to a nearby saguaro, a twenty-five footer. He looked at it, turned, and walked exactly ten paces. Then he turned again, brought up the shotgun, sighted on the cactus, and began to fire. He fired at its base over and over.

I put my hand to my mouth, shutting off a scream.

Hank fired again, and the cactus toppled.

It didn't fall like a man would if he were shot. It just leaned backwards. Then it gave a sort of sigh and leaned farther and farther. As it leaned, it picked up momentum, and, when it hit the ground, there as an awful thud.

Hank gave the cactus a satisfied nod and marched back toward his horse.

I found my voice. "Hey, you! Just what do you think you're doing?"

Hank got on the bay. "Cactuses are like people, Kathryn. They can't do anything for you once they're dead. Think about it."

"You bet I'll think about it! That cactus was valuable to me. You're going to pay!"

"What happens when there're no cactuses left?"

"What? What?"

"How're you going to scratch out a living on this miserable ranch if someone shoots all your cactuses?"

"You wouldn't dare!"

He smirked at me. "You know, there's one way cactuses *aren't* like people. Nobody ever hung a man for shooting one."

Then he rode off.

I stood there speechless. Did the bastard plan to shoot up my cacti until I agreed to marry him?

I went over to the saguaro. It lay on its back, oozing water. I nudged it gently with my foot. There were a few round holes in it—entrances to the caves where the Gila woodpeckers lived. From the silence, I guessed the birds hadn't been inside when the cactus toppled. They'd be mighty surprised when they came back and found their home on the ground.

The woodpeckers were the least of my problems, however. They'd just take up residence in one of the other giants. Trouble was, what if Hank carried out his veiled threat? Then the woodpeckers would run out of nesting places—and I'd run out of fruit to make my wine from.

I went back to the granddaddy of my cacti and picked up the basket. On the porch I set it down and myself in the rocking chair to think. What was I going to do?

I could go to the sheriff in Arroyo, but the idea didn't please me. For one thing, like Hank had said, there was no law against shooting a cactus. And for another, it was embarrassing to be in this kind of predicament at my age. I could see all the locals lining up at the bar of the saloon, laughing at me. No, I didn't want to go to Sheriff Daly if I could help it.

So what else? I could shoot Hank, I supposed, but that was even less appealing. Not that he didn't deserve shooting, but they could hang you for murdering a man, unlike a cactus. And then, while I had a couple of Joe's old rifles, I'd never been comfortable with them, never really mastered the art of sighting and pulling the trigger. With my luck, I'd miss Hank and kill off yet another cactus.

I sat on the porch for a long time, puzzling and listening to the night sounds of the desert. Finally I gave up and went to bed, hoping the old fool would come to his senses in the morning.

He didn't, though. Shotgun blasts on the far side of the ranch brought me flying out of the house the next night. By the time I got over there, there was nothing around except a couple of dead cacti. The next night it happened again, and still the next night. The bastard was being cagey, too. I had no way of proving it actually was Hank doing the shooting. Finally I gave up and decided I had no choice but to see Sheriff Daly.

I put on my good dress, fixed my hair, and hitched up my horse to the old buckboard. The trip into Arroyo was hot and dusty, and my stomach lurched at every bump in the road. It's no fun knowing you're about to become a laughingstock. Even if the sheriff sympathized with me, you can bet he and the boys would have a good chuckle afterwards.

I drove up Main Street, and left the rig at the livery stable. The horse needed shoeing anyway. Then I went down the wooden sidewalk to the sheriff's office. Naturally it was closed. The sign said he'd be back at two, and it was only noon now. I got out my list of errands and set off for the feed store, glancing over at the saloon on my way.

Hank was coming out of the saloon. I ducked into the shadow of the covered walkway in front of the bank and watched him, hate rising inside me. He stopped on the sidewalk and waited, and a moment later a stranger joined him. The stranger wore a frock coat and a broad-brimmed black hat. He didn't dress like anyone from these parts. Hank and the man walked toward the old adobe hotel and shook hands in front of it. Then Hank ambled over to where the bay was tied, and the stranger went inside.

I stood there, frowning. Normally I wouldn't have been curious about Hank Gardner's private business, but when a man's shooting up your cacti, you develop an interest in anything he does. I waited until he had ridden off down the street, then crossed and went into the hotel.

Sonny, the clerk, was a friend from 'way back. His mother and I had run church bazaars together for years, back when I still had the energy for that sort of thing. I went up to him, and we exchanged pleasantries.

Then I said: "Sonny, I've got a question for you, and I'd just as soon you didn't mention me asking it to anybody."

He nodded.

"A man came in here a few minutes ago. Frock coat, black hat."

"Sure. Mister Johnson."

"Who is he?"

"You don't know?"

"I don't get into town much these days."

"I guess not. Everybody's talking about him. Mister Johnson's a land developer. Here from Phoenix."

Land developer. I began to smell a rat. A rat named Hank Gardner.

"What's he doing, buying up the town?"

"Not the town. The countryside. He's making offers on all the ranches." Sonny eyed me thoughtfully. "Maybe you better talk to him. You've got a fair-sized spread there. You could make good money. In fact, I'm surprised he hasn't been out to see you."

"So am I, Sonny. So am I. You see him, you tell him I'd like to talk to him."

"He's in his room now. I could. . . ."

"No." I held up my hand. "I've got a lot of errands to do. I'll talk to him later."

But I didn't do my errands. Instead I went home to sit in my rocker and think.

That night I didn't light my kerosene lamp. I kept the house dark and waited at the front door. When the

20

evening darkness had fallen, I heard a rustling sound. A tall figure slipped around the stone wall into the dooryard.

I watched as he approached one of the giant saguaros in the dooryard. He went right up to it, like he had the first one he'd shot, turned, and walked exactly ten paces, then blasted away. The cactus toppled, and Hank ran from the yard.

I waited. Let him think I wasn't to home. After about fifteen minutes, I got undressed and went to bed in the dark, but I didn't rest much. My mind was too busy planning what I had to do.

The next morning I hitched up the buckboard and drove over to Hank's ranch. He was around back, mending a harness. He started when he saw me. Probably figured I'd come to shoot him. I got down from the buckboard and walked up to him, a sad, defeated look on my face.

"You're too clever for me, Hank. I should have known it."

"You ready to stop your foolishness and marry me?"

"Hank," I lied, "there's something more to my refusal than just stubbornness."

He frowned. "Oh?"

"Yes. You see, I promised Joe on his deathbed that I'd never marry again. That promise means something to me."

"I don't believe in. . . ."

"Hush. I've been thinking, though, about what you said about farming my ranch. I've got an idea. Why *don't* you farm it for me? I'll move in over here, keep house, and feed you. We're old enough everyone would know there weren't any shenanigans going on."

Hank looked thoughtful, pleased even. I'd guessed right; it wasn't my fair body he was after.

"That might work. But what if one of us died? Then what?"

"I don't see what you mean."

"Well, if you died, I'd be left with nothing to show for all that farming. And if I died, my son might come back from Tucson and throw you off the place. Where would you be then?"

"I see." I looked undecided, fingering a pleat in my skirt. "That is a problem." I paused. "Say, I think there's a way around it."

"Yeah?"

"Yes. We'll make wills. I'll leave you my ranch in mine. You do the same in yours. That way we'd both have something to show for our efforts."

He nodded, looking foxy. "That's a good idea, Kathryn. Very good." I could tell he was pleased I'd thought of it myself.

"And Hank, I think we should do it right away. Let's go into town this afternoon and have the wills drawn up."

"Fine with me." He looked even more pleased. "Just let me finish with this harness."

The will signing, of course, was a real solemn occasion. I even sniffed a little into my handkerchief before I put my signature to the document. The

22

lawyer, Will Jones, was a little surprised by our bequests, but not much. He knew I was alone in the world, and Hank's son John was known to be more of a ne'er-do-well than his father. Probably Will Jones was glad to see the ranch wouldn't be going to John.

I had Hank leave me off at my place on his way home. I wanted, I said, to cook him one last supper in my old house before moving to his in the morning. I went about my preparations, humming to myself. Would Hank be able to resist rushing back into town to talk to Johnson, the land developer? Or would he wait a decent interval, say a day?

Hank rode up around sundown. I met him on the porch, twisting my handkerchief in my hands.

"Kathryn, what's wrong?"

"Hank, I can't do it."

"Can't do what?"

"I can't leave the place. I can't leave Joe's memory. This whole thing's been a terrible mistake."

He scowled. "Don't be foolish. What's for supper?"

"There isn't any."

"What?"

"How could I fix supper with a terrible mistake like this on my mind?"

"Well, you just get in there and fix it. And stop talking this way."

I shook my head. "No, Hank, I mean it. I can't move to your place. I can't let you farm mine. It wouldn't be right. I want you to go now, and tomorrow I'm going into town to rip up my will."

"You what?" His eyes narrowed.

"You heard me, Hank."

He whirled and went toward his horse. "You'll never learn, will you?"

"What are you going to do?"

"What do you think? Once your damned cactuses are gone, you'll see the light. Once you can't make any more of that wine, you'll be only too glad to pack your bags and come with me."

"Hank, don't you dare!"

"I do dare. There won't be a one of them standing."

"Please, Hank! At least leave my granddaddy cactus." I waved at the fifty-foot giant in the outer dooryard. "It's my favorite. It's like a child to me."

Hank grinned evilly. He took the shotgun from the saddle and walked right up to the cactus.

"Say good bye to your child."

"Hank! Stop!"

He shouldered the shotgun.

"Say good bye to it, you foolish woman."

"Hank, don't pull that trigger!"

He pulled it.

Hank blasted at the giant saguaro—one, two, three times. And, like the others, it began to lean.

Unlike the others, though, it didn't lean backwards. It gave a great sigh and leaned and leaned and leaned forwards. And then it toppled. As it toppled, it picked up momentum. And when it fell on Hank Gardner, it made an awful thud.

I stood quietly on the porch. Hank didn't move.

24

Finally I went over to him. Dead. Dead as all the cacti he'd murdered.

I contemplated his broken body a bit before I hitched up the buckboard and went to tell Sheriff Daly about the terrible accident. Sure was funny, I'd say, how that cactus toppled forwards instead of backwards. Almost as if the base had been partly cut through and braced so it would do exactly that.

Of course, the shotgun blasts would have destroyed any traces of the cutting.

The Sanchez Sacraments

I was in the basement of the museum unpacking the pottery figures Adolpho Sanchez had left us when I began to grow puzzled about the old man and his work. It was the priest figures that bothered me.

Sanchez had been one of Mexico's most outstanding folk artists, living in seclusion near the pottery-making center of Metepec. His work had taken the form of groupings of figures participating in such religious ceremonies as weddings, feast days, and baptisms. The figures we'd received from his estate—actually from the executrix of his estate, his sister, Lucia—represented an entire life cycle in five of the seven Catholic sacraments. They'd arrived by truck only yesterday, along with Sanchez's written instructions about setting them up, and I'd decided to devote this morning to unpacking them so we could place them on display in our special exhibits gallery next week.

The crate I'd started with contained the priests, one for each sacrament, and I'd set the two-foot-tall, highly glazed pottery figures at intervals around the room, waiting to be joined by the other figures that would complete each scene. Four of the five figures represented the same man, his clean-shaven face dour, eyes kindly and wise. The fifth, which belonged to the depiction of extreme unction—The Last Rites—was bearded and haggard, with an expression of great pain.

26

But what was puzzling was that this priest was holding out a communion wafer, presumably to a dying parishioner.

I'm not a practicing Catholic, in spite of the fact I was raised one, but I do remember enough of my Catechism to know that they don't give communion during extreme unction. What they do is anoint the sense organs with body oil. Adolfo Sanchez certainly should have known that, too, because he was an extremely devout Catholic and devoted his life to portraying religious scenes such as this.

There was a book on the worktable that I'd bought on the old man's life and works. I flipped through it to see if there were any pictures of other scenes depicting extreme unction, but, if he'd done any, there weren't any in this particular volume. Disappointed, I skimmed backwards through a section of pictures of the artist and his family and found the biographical sketch at the front of the book.

Adolfo had been born seventy-seven years ago in Metepec. As was natural for a local boy with artistic talent, he'd taken up the potter's trade. He'd married late, in his mid-thirties, to a local girl named Constantina Lopez, and they'd had one child, Rosalinda. Rosalinda had married late, also, by Mexican standards— in her early twenties—and had given birth to twin boys two years later. Constantina Sanchez had died shortly after her grandsons' birth, and Rosalinda had followed, after a lingering illness, when the twins were five. Ever since the boys had left home, Adolfo had lived in seclusion with only his sister Lucia as faithful companion. He had devoted himself to his art, even to the point of never attending church.

Maybe, I thought, he'd stayed away long enough that he'd forgotten exactly how things were done in the Catholic faith. But I'd stayed away, and I still remembered.

Senility, then? I flipped to the photograph of the old man at the front of the book and stared into his eyes, clear and alert above his finely chiseled nose and thick beard. No, Sanchez had not been senile. Well, in any event, it was time I got on with unpacking the rest of the figures.

I was cradling one of a baptismal infant when Emily, my secretary, appeared. She stood at the bottom of the steps, one hand on the newel post, her pale-haired head cocked to one side, looking worried.

"Elena?" she said. "There are two . . . gentlemen here to see you."

Something about the way she said "gentlemen" gave me pause. I set the infant's figure down on the work-table. "What gentlemen?"

"The Sanchez brothers."

"Who?" For a moment I didn't connect them with the twins I'd just been reading about. Sanchez is a common Mexican name.

"They're here about the pottery." She motioned at the crates. "One is in your office, and Susana has taken the other to the courtyard."

Susana Ibarra was the Museum of Mexican Arts'

public relations director—and troubleshooter. If she had elected to take one of the Sanchez twins under her wing, it was because he was either upset or about to cause a scene.

"Is everything all right?"

Emily shrugged. "So far."

"I'll be right up."

"Which one do you want to see first?"

"Can I see them together?"

"I wouldn't advise it. They almost came to blows in the courtyard before Susana took over."

"Oh." I paused. "Well, then, if Susana has the one she's talking to under control, I'll go directly to my office."

Emily nodded and went upstairs.

I moved the infant's figure into the center of the large worktable and checked to see if the other figures were securely settled. To break one of them would destroy the effect of the entire work, to say nothing of its value. When I'd assured myself they were safe, I followed Emily upstairs.

Once there, I hurried through the folk art gallery, with its Tree of Life and colorful paper-mâché animals, and peered out into the central courtyard. Susana Ibarra and a tall man wearing jeans and a rough cotton shirt stood near the little fountain. The man's arms were folded across his chest and he was frowning down at her. Susana had her hands on her hips and was tossing her thick mane of black hair for emphasis as she spoke. From the aggressive way she balanced on her high heels, I could tell that she was giving the man a lecture. And, knowing Susana, if that didn't work, she'd probably dunk him in the fountain. Reassured, I smiled and went to the office wing.

When I stepped into my office, the young man seated in the visitor's chair jumped to his feet. He was as tall as Susana's companion, and had the same lean, chiseled features and short black hair. In his light tan suit, conservative tie, and highly polished shoes, he looked excessively formal for the casual atmosphere of Santa Barbara.

I held out my hand and said: "Mister Sanchez? I'm Elena Oliverez, director of the museum."

"Gilberto Sanchez." His accent told me he was a Mexican national. He paused, then added: "Adolfo Sanchez's grandson."

"Please, sit down." I went around the desk and took my padded leather chair. "I understand you're here about the Sacraments."

For a moment he looked blank. "Oh, the figures from *Tía* Lucia. Yes."

"You didn't know they're called the Sanchez Sacraments?"

"No. I didn't know anything about them. That is why I'm here."

"I don't understand."

He leaned forward, his fine features serious. "Let me explain. My mother died when my brother Eduardo and I were only five . . . we are fraternal twins. My father had left long before that, so we had only Grandfather and *Tía* Lucia. But Grandfather wanted us to see more of the world than Metepec. It is a small town, and Grandfather's village is even smaller. So he sent us to school and then university in Mexico City. After college I remained on there."

"So you never saw the Sacraments?"

"No. I knew Grandfather was working on something important the last years of his life, but, whenever I went to visit him, he refused to let me see the project. It was the same with Eduardo . . . we were not even allowed in his workroom."

"Did he tell you anything about it?"

"No. *Tía* Lucia did not even know. All she said was that he had told her it was the finish of his life's work. Now he is gone, and, even before Eduardo and I could get to Metepec for the funeral, *Tía* Lucia shipped the figures off to you. She won't talk about them, just says they are better off in a museum."

"And you . . . ?"

"I want to see them. Surely you can understand that, Miss Oliverez. I loved my grandfather. Somehow it will make his death easier to accept if I can see the work of the last ten years of his life." Gilberto's eyes shone with emotion as he spoke.

I nodded, tapping my fingers on the arm of my chair. It was an odd story, and it sounded as if Gilberto's aunt hadn't wanted him or his twin brother to see the figures. To give myself time to order my thoughts, I said: "What do you do in Mexico City, Mister Sanchez?"

If the abrupt switch in subject surprised him, he didn't show it. "I am a banker."

That explained his conservative dress. "I see."

He smiled suddenly, a wonderful smile that transformed his face and showed me what he might be like without the pall of death hanging over him. "Oh, I am not totally without the family madness, as my grandfather used to call the artistic temperament. I paint in my spare time."

"Oils?'

"Yes."

"Are you talented?"

He considered. "Yes, I think so."

I liked his candor, and immediately decided I also liked him. "Mister Sanchez, I understand you and your brother almost came to blows in our courtyard earlier."

The smile dropped away and he colored slightly. "Yes, we met as we were both coming in. I had no idea he was in Santa Barbara."

"What was your argument about?"

"The Sacraments, as you call them. You see, Eduardo also came to Metepec for the funeral. He lives in Chicago now, where he is a filmmaker . . . television commercials mainly, but he also does other, more artistic work. The family madness passed down to him, too. Anyway, he was as upset as I was about the Sacraments being gone, but for a different reason."

"And what was that?"

Gilberto laced his long fingers together and looked

down at them, frowning. "He thinks *Tía* Lucia had no right to give them away. He says they should have come down to us. And he wants them back so he can sell them."

"And you don't agree?"

"No, I don't." Quickly he looked up. "We were well provided for in Grandfather's will, but he made *Tía* Lucia his executrix. She says it was Grandfather's wish that the Sacraments go to a museum. And I feel a man has the right to dispose of his work in any way he chooses."

"Then why are you here?"

"Only because I wish to see the Sacraments."

I decided right then that I had better contact Lucia Sanchez before I went any further with this. "Well, Mister Sanchez," I said, "the figures just arrived yesterday and haven't been unpacked yet. I plan to have them on exhibit early next week. At that time. . . ."

"Would it be possible for me to view them privately?"

He looked so eager that I hated to disappoint him, so I said: "I'm sure something can be arranged."

The smile spread across his face again, and he got to his feet. "I would appreciate that very much."

Aware that he would not want another run-in with his brother, I showed him the way out through the little patio outside my office, then started out to the central courtyard. Emily was at her desk, doing something to a ditto master with a razor blade.

"Is Susana still talking to Eduardo Sanchez?" I asked her.

"Yes. They seem to have made friends. At least they were sitting on the edge of the fountain laughing when I went past five minutes ago."

"Susana could charm the spots off a leopard." I turned to go, then paused. "Emily, do we have a telephone number for Lucia Sanchez?"

"Yes, I put it in my Rolodex."

"I'll want to talk to her today."

"Then I'd better start trying now. Service to the Metepec area is bound to be poor."

"Right. If I'm not back here by the time the call goes through, come and get me." I turned and went through the doorway to the courtyard.

As Emily had said, Susana and Eduardo Sanchez were sitting on the edge of the blue-tiled fountain, and she appeared to be telling him one of her infamous jokes. Susana loved long jokes, the more complicated the better. The trouble was, she usually forgot the punch lines, or mixed them up with the endings of other jokes. Only her prettiness and girlish charm—she was only seventeen—saved her from mayhem at the hands of her listeners.

When he saw me, Eduardo Sanchez stood up—not as quickly as his brother had, but almost indolently. Up close I could see that his fine features were chiseled more sharply than Gilberto's, as if the sculptor had neglected to smooth off the rough edges. His hair was longer, too, artfully blow-dried, and, although his attire was casual, I noted his loafers were Gucci.

Eduardo's handshake, when Susana introduced us,

was indolent, too. His accent was not so pronounced as his twin's, and I thought I caught a faint, incongruous touch of the Midwest in the way he said hello.

I said: "It's a pleasure to meet you, Mister Sanchez. I see Miz Ibarra has been taking good care of you."

He glanced over at Susana, who was standing, smoothing the pleats of her bright green dress. "Yes, she has been telling me a story about a dog who dresses up as a person in order to get the fire department to 'rescue' a cat he has chased up a tree. We have not reached the ending, however, and I fear we never will."

Susana flashed her brilliant smile. "Can I help it if I forget? The jokes are all very long, and in this life a person can only keep so much knowledge in her head."

"Don't worry, Susana," I said. "I'd rather you kept the dates of our press releases in there than the punch line to such a silly story."

"Speaking of the press releases. . . ." She turned and went toward the door to the office wing.

Eduardo Sanchez's eyes followed her. "An enchanting girl," he said.

"Yes, we're fortunate to have her on staff. And now, what can I do for you? I assume you've come about the Sacraments?"

Unlike his brother, he seemed to know what they were called. "Yes. Has Gilberto filled you in?"

"A little."

Eduardo reclaimed his seat on the edge of the fountain. "He probably painted me as quite the villain, too.

35

But at least you know why I'm here. Those figures should never have been donated to this museum. Rightfully they belong to Gilberto and me. We either want them returned or paid for."

"You say 'we'. It was my impression that all your brother wants is to see them."

He made an impatient gesture with one hand. "For a banker Gilberto isn't very smart."

"But he does seem to have respect for your grandfather's wishes. He loved him very much, you know."

His eyes flashed angrily. "And do you think I didn't? I worshipped the man. If it wasn't for him and his guidance, I'd be nobody today."

"Then why go against his wishes?"

"For the simple reason that I don't know if donating those pieces to this museum was what he wanted."

"You think your aunt made that up?"

"She may have."

"Why?"

"I don't know!" He got up and began to pace.

I hesitated, then framed my words carefully. "Mister Sanchez, I think you have come to the wrong person about this. It appears to be a family matter, one you should work out with your aunt and brother."

"I have tried."

"Try again. Because there's really nothing I can do."

His body tensed, and he swung around to face me. I tensed, too, ready to step back out of his reach. But then he relaxed with a conscious effort, and a lazy· smile spread across his face.

"Clever, aren't you?"

"I have to be, Mister Sanchez. The art world may seem gentle and non-materialistic to outsiders, but . . . as you know from your work in films . . . art is as cut-throat as any other. To run a museum, you have to be clever . . . and strong-willed."

"I get your message." The smile did not leave his face.

"Then you'll discuss this with your family?"

"Among others. I'll be in touch." He turned and stalked out of the courtyard.

I stood there, surprised he'd given up so easily, and very much on my guard. Eduardo Sanchez was not going to go away. Nor was his brother. As if I didn't have enough to contend with here at the museum, now I would be dragged into a family quarrel. Sighing, I went to see if Emily had been able to put my call through to Metepec.

The following afternoon, Lucia Sanchez sat across my desk from me, her dark eyes focused anxiously on mine. In her cotton dress that was faded from too many washings, her work-roughened hands clutching a shabby leather handbag, she reminded me of the aunts of my childhood who would come from Mexico for family weddings or funerals. They had seemed like people from another century, those silent women who whispered among themselves and, otherwise, spoke only when spoken to. It had been hard to imagine them as young or impassioned, and it was the same with Miss Sanchez. Only her eyes seemed truly alive.

When I'd spoken to her on the phone the day before, she'd immediately been alarmed at her great-nephews' presence in Santa Barbara and had decided to come to California to reason with them.

Now she said: "Have you heard anything further from either of the boys?"

"Oh, yes." I nodded. "Gilberto has called twice today asking when the figures will be ready for viewing. Eduardo has also called twice, threatening to retain a lawyer if I don't either return the Sacraments or settle upon a 'mutually acceptable price'."

Lucia Sanchez made a disgusted sound. "This is what it comes to. After all their grandfather and I did for them."

"I can see where you would be upset by Eduardo's behavior, but what Gilberto is asking seems quite reasonable."

"You do not know the whole story. Tell me, are the figures on display yet?"

"They have been arranged in our special exhibits gallery, yes. But it will not be open to the public until next Monday."

"Good." She nodded and stood, and the calm decisiveness of her manner at once erased all resemblance to my long-departed aunts. "I should like to see the pieces, if I may."

I got up and led her from the office wing and across the courtyard to the gallery that held our special exhibits. I'd worked all the previous afternoon and evening setting up the figures with the help of two student volunteers from my alma mater, the University of California's Santa Barbara campus. This sort of active participation in creating the exhibits was not the usual province of a director, but we were a small museum and, since our director had been murdered and I'd been promoted last spring, we'd had yet to find a curator who would work for the equally small salary we could offer. These days I wore two hats—not always comfortably.

Now, as I ushered Lucia Sanchez into the gallery and turned on the overhead spotlights, I had to admit that the late evening I'd put in had been worthwhile. There were five groupings, each on a raised platform, each representing a sacrament. The two-foot-tall pottery figures were not as primitive in appearance as most folk art; instead, they were highly representational, with perfect proportions and expressive faces. Had they not been fired in an extremely glossy and colorful glaze, they would have seemed almost real.

Lucia Sanchez paused on the threshold of the room, then began moving counterclockwise, studying the figures. I followed.

The first Sacrament was a baptism, the father holding the infant before the priest while the mother and friends and relatives looked on. Next came a confirmation, the same proud parents beaming in the background. The figure of the bride in the wedding ceremony was so carefully crafted that I felt if I reached out and touched her dress, it would be the traditional embroidered cotton, rather than clay. The father smiled broadly as he gave her away, placing her hand in that of the groom.

The other two groupings were not of joyous occasions. Extreme unction—The Last Rites—involved only the figure of the former bride on her deathbed and the priest, oddly offering her the final communion wafer. And the last scene—Penance—was not a grouping either, but merely the figure of a man kneeling in the confessional, the priest's face showing dimly through the grille. Logically the order of these two scenes should have been reversed, but Sanchez's written instructions for setting them up had indicated it should be done in this order.

Lucia Sanchez circled the room twice, stopping for a long time in front of each of the scenes. Then, looking shaken, she returned to where I stood near the door and pushed past me into the courtyard. She went to the edge of the fountain and stood there for a long moment, hands clasped on her purse, head bowed, staring into the splashing water. Finally I went up beside her and touched her arm.

"Miss Sanchez," I said, "are you all right?"

She continued staring down for about ten seconds, then raised agonized eyes to mine. "Miss Oliverez," she said, "you must help me."

"With the possibility of a lawsuit? Of course. . . ."

"No, not just the lawsuit. That is not really important. But I do ask your help with this . . . Gilberto and Eduardo must never see those figures. Never, do you understand? Never!"

40

At nine o'clock that evening, I was sitting in the living room of my little house in Santa Barbara's flatlands, trying to read a fat adventure novel Susana had loaned me. It was hot for late September, and I wore shorts and had the windows open for cross-ventilation. An hour before the sound of the neighbors' kids playing kickball in the street had been driving me crazy; now everything seemed too quiet.

The phone hadn't rung once all evening. My current boy friend—Dave Kirk, an Anglo homicide cop, of all things—was mad at me for calling off a tentative date the previous evening so I could set up the Sanchez Sacraments. My mother, who usually checked in at least once a day to make sure I was still alive and well, was off on a cruise with her seventy-eight-year-old boy friend. Although her calls normally made me think a move to Nome, Alaska, would be desirable, now I missed her and would have liked to hear her voice.

I also would have liked to talk out the matter of the Sanchez Sacraments with her. Mama had a keen intelligence and an ability to see things sometimes I'd missed that were right under my nose. And in the case of the Sacraments, I was missing something very important. Namely why Lucia Sanchez was so adamant that neither of her great-nephews should ever view the figures.

Try as I might, I hadn't been able to extract the reason from her that afternoon. So, perversely, I hadn't promised that I would bar the brothers from the gallery. I honestly didn't see how I could keep them away from a public exhibit, but perhaps, had I known Lucia's reason, I might have been more willing to find a way. As it was, I felt trapped between the pleas of this woman, who I liked very much, and the well-reasoned request of Gilberto. And on top of that, there was the fear of a lawsuit over the Sacraments. I hadn't been able to talk to the museum's attorney—he was on vacation—and I didn't want to do anything, such as refusing the brothers access to the exhibit, which would make Eduardo's claim against us stronger.

I shifted on the couch and propped my feet on the coffee table, crossing them at the ankles. I gave the novel a final cursory glance, sighed, and tossed it aside. Susana and I simply did not have the same taste in fiction. There was a *Sunset* magazine that she had also given me on the end table. Normally I wouldn't have looked at a publication that I considered aimed at trendy, affluent Anglos, but now I picked it up and began to thumb through it. I was reading an article on outdoor decking—ridiculous, because my house needed a paint job far more than backyard beautification—when the phone rang. I jumped for it.

The caller was Lucia Sanchez. "I hope I am not disturbing you by calling so late, Miss Oliverez."

"No, not at all."

"I wanted to tell you that I had dinner with Gilberto and Eduardo. They remain adamant about seeing the Sacraments."

"So Eduardo now wants to see them, also?"

"Yes. I assume so he can assess their value." Her tone was weary and bitter.

I was silent.

"Miss Oliverez," she said, "what can we do?"

I felt a prickle of annoyance at her use of the word "we". "I don't suppose there's anything you can do. *I*, however, can merely stall them until I speak with the museum's attorney. But I think he'll merely advise me to let them see the figures."

"That must not be!"

"I don't know what else to do. Perhaps if I knew your reason. . . ."

"We have discussed that before. It is a reason rooted in the past. I wish to let the past die, as my brother died."

"Then there's nothing I can do but follow the advice of our lawyer."

She made a sound that could have been a sob, and abruptly hung up. I clutched the receiver, feeling cruel and tactless. The woman obviously had a strong reason for what she was asking, so strong that she could confide in no one. And the reason had to be in those figures. Something I could see but hadn't interpreted. . . .

I decided to go to the museum and take a close look at the Sanchez Sacraments.

The old adobe building that housed the museum gleamed whitely in its floodlights. I drove around and parked my car in the lot, then entered by the loading dock, resetting the alarm system behind me. After switching on the lights, I crossed the courtyard—silent now, the fountain's merry tinkling stilled for the night—and went into the special exhibits gallery.

The figures stood frozen in time—celebrants at three rites and sufferers at two others. I turned up the spots to full beam and began with the baptismal scene.

Father, mother, aunts and uncles, and cousins and friends. A babe in arms, white dress trimmed with pink ribbons. Priest, the one with the long jaw and dour lines around his mouth. Father was handsome, with chiseled features, reminiscent of the Sanchez brothers. Mother, conventionally pretty. All the participants had the wonderfully expressive faces that had been Adolfo Sanchez's trademark. Many reminded me, as Lucia had initially, of my relatives from Mexico.

Confirmation. Daughter kneeling before the same priest. Conventionally pretty, like her mother who looked on. Father proud, hand on wife's shoulder. Again, the relatives and friends.

Wedding ceremony. Pretty daughter grown into a young woman. Parents somewhat aged, but prouder than ever. Bridegroom in first flush of manhood. Same family and friends and priest—also slightly aged.

So far I saw nothing but the work of an exceptionally talented artist who deserved the international acclaim he had received.

Deathbed scene. Formerly pretty daughter, not so much aged as withered by illness. No family, friends. Priest—the different one, bearded, his features wracked with pain as he offered the communion wafer. The pain was similar to that in the dying woman's eyes. This figure had disturbed me. . . .

I stared at it for a minute, then went on.

Penance. A man, his face in his hands. Leaning on the ledge in the confessional, telling his sins. The priest—the one who had officiated at the first joyful rites—was not easily visible through the grille, but I could make out the look of horror on his face that I had first noted when I unpacked the figure.

I stared at the priest's face for a long time, then went back to the deathbed scene. The other priest knelt by the bed. . . .

There was a sudden, stealthy noise outside. I whirled and listened. It came again, from the entryway. I went out into the courtyard and saw light flickering briefly over the little windows to either side of the door.

I relaxed, smiling a little. I knew who this was. Our ever-vigilant Santa Barbara police had noticed a light on where one should not be and were checking to make sure no one was burglarizing the museum. This had happened so often—because I worked late frequently—that they didn't bother to creep up as softly as they might. If I had been a burglar, by now I could have been in the next county. As it was, I'd seen so much of these particular cops that I was considering offering them an honorary membership in our museum society. Still, I appreciated their alertness. With a sigh, I went back and switched out the spots in the gallery, then crossed the courtyard to assure them all was well.

45

・・・

A strong breeze came up around three in the morning. It ruffled the curtains at my bedroom window and made the single sheet covering me inadequate. I pulled it higher on my shoulders and curled myself into a ball, too tired to reach down to the foot of the bed for the blanket. In moments I drifted back into a restless sleep, haunted by images of people at religious ceremonies. Or were they people? They stood too still, their expressions were too fixed. Expressions—of joy, of pain, of horror. Pain . . . horror. . . .

Suddenly the dream was gone and I sat up in bed, remembering the one thing that had disturbed me about Adolfo Sanchez's deathbed scene—and realizing another. I fumbled for the light, found my robe, and went barefooted into the living room to the bookcase where I kept my art library. Somewhere I had that book on Adolfo's life and works, the one I'd bought when the Sacraments had been donated to the museum. I'd barely had time to glance through it again.

There were six shelves, and I scanned each impatiently. Where was the damned book anyway? Then I remembered it was at the museum; I'd looked through it in the basement the other day. As far as I knew, it was still on the worktable.

I stood, clutching my robe around me, and debated going to the museum to get the book. But it was not a good time to be on the streets alone, even in a relatively crime-free town like Santa Barbara, and, besides, I'd already alarmed the police once tonight. Better to look at the book when I went in at the regular time next morning.

I went back to bed, pulling the blanket up, and huddled there, thinking about death and penance.

I arrived at the museum early next morning—at eight o'clock, an hour before my usual time. When I entered the office wing, I could hear a terrific commotion going on in the central courtyard. People were yelling in Spanish, all at once, not bothering to listen to one another. I recognized Susana's voice, and thought I heard Lucia Sanchez. The other voices were male, and I could guess they belonged to the Sanchez brothers. They must have used some ploy to get Susana to let them in this early.

I hurried through the offices and out into the courtyard. Susana turned when she heard my footsteps, her face flushed with anger. "Elena," she said, "you must do something about them!"

The others merely went on yelling. I had been right. It was Gilberto, Eduardo, and Lucia, and they were right in the middle of one of those monumental quarrels that my people are famous for.

". . . contrived to steal our heritage, and I will not allow it!" This from Eduardo.

"You were amply taken care of in your grandfather's will. And now you want more. Greed!" Lucia shook a finger at him.

"I merely want what is mine."

47

"Yours!" Lucia looked as if she might spit at him.

"Yes, mine."

"What about Gilberto? Have you forgotten him?"

Eduardo glanced at his brother, who was cowering by the fountain. "No, of course not. The proceeds from the Sacraments will be divided equally. . . ."

"I don't want the money!" Gilberto said.

"You be quiet!" Eduardo turned on him. "You are too foolish to know what's good for you. You could help me convince this old witch, but instead you're mooning around here, protesting that you *only want to see* the Sacraments." His voice cruelly mimicked Gilberto. "But you will receive the money set aside for you in Grandfather's will. . . ."

"It's not enough."

"Not enough for what?"

"I must finish my life's work."

"What work?"

"My film."

"I thought the film was done."

Eduardo looked away. "We ran over budget."

"A-hah! You've already squandered your inheritance. Before you've received it, it's spent. And now you want more. Greed!"

"My film. . . ."

"Film, film, film! I am tired of hearing about it."

This had all been very interesting, but I decided it was time to intervene. Just as Eduardo gave a howl of wounded indignation, I said in Spanish: "All right! That's enough!"

48

All three turned to me, as if they hadn't known I was there. At once they looked embarrassed; in their family, as in mine, quarrels should be kept strictly private.

I looked at Lucia. "Miss Sanchez, I want to see you in my office." Then I motioned at the brothers. "You two leave. If I catch you on the premises again without my permission, I'll have you jailed for trespassing."

They grumbled and glowered but moved toward the door. Susana followed, making shooing gestures.

I turned and led Lucia Sanchez to the office wing. When she was seated in my visitor's chair, I said: "Wait here. I'll be back in a few minutes." Then I went downstairs to the basement. The book I'd been looking for the night before was where I'd left it earlier in the week, on the worktable. I opened it and leafed through to the section of pictures of the artist and his family.

When young, Adolfo Sanchez had had the same chiseled features as his grandsons; he had, however, been handsome in a way they were not. In his later years, he had sported a beard, and his face had been deeply lined, his eyes sunken with pain.

I turned the page and found photographs of the family members. The wife, Constantina, was conventionally pretty. The daughter, Rosalinda, took after her mother. In a couple of the photographs, Lucia looked on in the background. A final one showed Adolfo with his arms around the two boys, age about six. Neither the wife nor the daughter was in evidence.

49

I shut the book with shaky hands, a sick feeling in the pit of my stomach. I should go to the special exhibits gallery and confirm my suspicions, but I didn't have the heart for it. Besides, the Sacraments were as clear in my mind as if I'd been looking at them. I went instead to my office.

Lucia Sanchez sat as she had before, roughened hands gripping her shabby leather bag. When I came in, she looked up and seemed to see the knowledge in my eyes. Wearily she passed a hand over her face.

"Yes," I said, "I've figured it out."

"Then you understand why the boys must never see those figures."

I sat down on the edge of the desk in front of her. "Why didn't you just tell me?"

"I've told no one, all those years. It was a secret between my brother and myself. But he had to expiate it, and he chose to do so through his work. I never knew what he was doing out there in his studio. The whole time, he refused to tell me. You can imagine my shock after he died, when I went to look and saw he'd told the whole story in his pottery figures."

"Of course, no one would guess, unless. . . ."

"Unless they knew the family history and what the members had looked like."

"Or noticed something was wrong with the figures and then studied photographs, like I just did."

She acknowledged it with a small nod.

"Adolfo and his wife had a daughter, Rosalinda," I said. "She's the daughter in the Sacraments, and the parents are Adolfo and Constantina. The resemblance is easy to spot."

"It's remarkable, isn't it . . . how Adolfo could make the figures so real. Most folk artists don't, you know." She spoke in a detached tone.

"And remarkable how he could make the scenes reflect real life."

"That, too." But now the detachment was gone, and pain crossed her face.

"Rosalinda grew up and married and had the twins. What happened to her husband?"

"He deserted her, even before the boys were born."

"And Constantina died shortly after."

"Yes. That was when I moved in with them, to help Rosalinda with the children. She was ill. . . ."

"Fatally ill. What was it?"

"Cancer."

"A painful illness."

"Yes."

"When did Adolfo decide to end her misery?"

She sat very still, white-knuckled hands clasping her purse.

"Did you know what he had done?" I asked.

Tears came into her eyes and one spilled over. She made no move to wipe it away. "I knew. But it was not as it seems. Rosalinda begged him to help her end her life. She was in such pain. How could Adolfo refuse his child's last request? All her life, she had asked so little of anyone. . . ."

"So he complied with her wishes. What did he give her?"

51

"An overdose of medicine for the pain. I don't know what kind."

"And then?"

"Gradually he began to fail. He was severely depressed. After a year he sent the boys to boarding school in Mexico City . . . such a sad household was no place for children, he said. For a while I feared he might take his own life, but then he began to work on those figures, and it saved him. He had a purpose and, I realize now, a penance to perform."

"And when the figures were finished, he died."

"Within days."

I paused, staring at her face, which was now streaked with tears. "He told me the whole story in the Sacraments . . . Rosalinda's baptism, confirmation, and marriage. The same friends and relatives were present, and the same parish priest."

"Father Rivera."

"But in the scene of extreme unction . . . Rosalinda's death . . . Father Rivera doesn't appear. Instead, the priest is Adolfo, and what he is handing Rosalinda appears to be a communion wafer. I noticed that as soon as I saw the figure and wondered about it, because for the last rites they don't give communion, they use holy oil. And it isn't supposed to be a wafer, either, but a lethal dose of pain medicine. At first I didn't notice the priest's resemblance to the father in the earlier scenes because of the beard. But when I really studied the photographs of Adolfo, it all became clear."

"That figure is the least representational of the lot,"

Lucia said. "I suppose Adolfo felt he couldn't portray his crime openly. He never wanted the boys to know. And he probably didn't want the world to know, either. Adolfo was a proud man, with an artist's pride in his work and reputation."

"I understand. If the story came out, it would tarnish the value of his work with sensationalism. He disguised himself in the penance scene, too, by having his hands over his face."

Lucia was weeping into her handkerchief now. Through it she said: "What are we going to do? Both of the boys are now determined to see the Sacraments. And when they do, they will interpret them as you have and despise Adolfo's memory. That was the one thing he feared . . . he said so in his will."

I got up, went to the little barred window that overlooked the small patio outside my office, and stood there staring absently at the azalea bushes that our former director had planted. I pictured Gilberto, as he'd spoken of his grandfather the other day, his eyes shining with love. And I heard Eduardo saying: "I worshipped the man. If it wasn't for his guidance, I'd be nobody today." They might understand what had driven Adolfo to his mortal sin, but if they didn't. . . .

Finally I said: "Perhaps we can do something, after all."

"But what? The figures will be on public display. And the boys are determined."

I felt a tension building inside me. "Let me deal with that problem."

My hands balled into fists, I went through the office wing and across the courtyard to the gallery. Once inside, I stopped, looking around at the figures. They were a perfect series of groupings, and they told a tale far more powerful than the simple life cycle I'd first taken them to represent. I wasn't sure I could do what I'd intended. What I was contemplating was—for a curator and an art lover—almost as much of a sin as Adolfo's helping his daughter kill herself.

I went over to the deathbed scene and rested my hand gently on the shoulder of the kneeling man. The figure was so perfect it felt almost real.

I thought of the artist, the man who had concealed his identity under these priestly robes. Wasn't the artist and the life he'd lived as important as his work? Part of my job was to protect those works; couldn't I also interpret that to mean I should also protect the memory of the artist?

I stood there for a long moment—and then I pushed the pottery figure, hard. It toppled backward, off the low platform to the stone floor. Pottery smashes easily, and this piece broke into many fragments. I stared down at them, wanting to cry.

When I came out of the gallery minutes later, Susana was rushing across the courtyard. "Elena, what happened? I heard. . . ." She saw the look on my face and stopped, one hand going to her mouth.

Keeping my voice steady, I said: "There's been an accident, and there's a mess on the floor of the gallery. Please get someone to clean it up. And after that, go to my office and tell Lucia Sanchez she and her great-nephews can view the Sacraments any time. Arrange a private showing for as long as they want. After all, they're family."

"What about . . . ?" She motioned at the gallery.

"Tell them one of the figures . . . Father Rivera, in the deathbed scene . . . was irreparably damaged in transit." I started toward the entryway.

"Elena, where are you going?"

"I'm taking the day off. You're in charge."

I would get away from here, maybe walk on the beach. I was fortunate; mine was only a small murder. I would not have to live with it or atone for it the remainder of my lifetime, as Adolfo Sanchez had.

Cave of Ice

On the hottest day of summer in the year 1901, Will Reese disobeyed his father's orders and returned to the ice cave. He just couldn't stay away any longer. He had thought about little else but the cave for the past week.

The entrance was at the bottom of a deep, rock-strewn depression on his folks' sheep ranch, one of many such pits in this section of the southern Idaho plain. His father had told him they were collapsed lava cones that had been formed by long-ago flows from the extinct volcano nearby. As Will climbed down into the depression, the temperature dropped with amazing swiftness. At the bottom, near the cave opening, the air had a wintry feel. The coldness was what had led him to the cave that day last week, after he had come here on the trail of a stray Hampshire yearling.

Will donned his sheepskin coat, lit the lantern he had brought, and wedged his tall, lank frame through the fissure into the cave's main chamber. When he stood up, the light reflected in dazzling pinpoints from a hundred icy surfaces.

Ice filled the cave, from frozen pools along its floor to huge crystals suspended from its ceiling twenty feet above. A massive glacial wall bulked up directly ahead, a wall that might have been a few feet or many yards thick. Several natural stone steps, sheeted with ice, led up to a narrow ledge nearby. On the ledge's far side was an icefall, a natural slide that dropped fifteen feet into an arched lava tube. At the bottom of the slide was a jumble of gleaming bones, probably those of a large animal that had fallen down the slide and been unable to climb out.

Will could see his breath misting frostily into the lamplight. He could hear water dripping into the cave from underground streams, water that would soon be frozen. He felt the same excitement he had the first time he'd stood here. An ice cave! He hadn't known such things existed. But his father had; Clay Reese had an unquenchable thirst for knowledge, which he tried to slake by reading and rereading mail-order books on many different subjects. He had told Will about the caves, after Will had raced home with news of his find and brought his father back.

There were two kinds of ice caves, one type found in glaciers and the other in volcanic fissures such as this one. Usually the ice in both types melted in warm weather, but this was one of the rare exceptions. No one knew for sure how or why such caves acted as natural icehouses. Perhaps it had something to do with air pressure and wind flow. The phenomenon was very rare, which made Will's discovery all the more special to him.

His father, however, hadn't seemed to understand this. "I don't want you coming back here again," he'd said. "Now don't argue, Son. It's not safe in a cave like this . . . all kinds of things can happen. Stay clear."

Will had tried in vain to get his father to change his

mind. Clay Reese was sometimes difficult to talk to, and lately he had been even more reticent than usual, as if something were weighing on his mind. A fiercely proud man, he had once dreamed of attending college, a dream that had ended with the death of his own father when he was Will's age, fifteen. Disappointment and hard work had turned him into a private person. Yet he and Will had always shared a closeness based on fairness and understanding. Until now, he had always listened to Will's side of things. Will just didn't understand the sudden change in him.

Will spent the better part of an hour exploring. Between the ice wall and the near lava wall was a passage that led more than fifty yards deeper under the volcanic rock, before it ended finally in a glacial barrier that completely filled the cave. Small chambers formed by arches and broken-rock walls opened off the passage. The cave was enormous, no telling yet just how large.

But an hour was all he could spare. He would be missed if he stayed much longer, and he had already been reprimanded more than once this week for neglecting his chores. He made his way back to the main chamber and slipped outside, shrugging out of his coat.

The summer heat was intense after the cave's chill; Will was sweating by the time he reached the rim of the pit. He started toward where he had left his roan horse picketed in the shade of a lava overhang. But then he stopped and stood shading his eyes, peering out over the flat, sun-blasted plain.

Billows of dust rose in a long line, hazing the bright blue sky. Wagons, four of them, were coming from the direction of Volcano, the only settlement within twenty miles. They weren't traveling on the road that led out among the sheep ranches in the area; they were coming at an angle through the sagebrush. And they seemed to be heading toward Will.

Frowning, he moved over next to his horse and waited there, hidden, holding the animal's muzzle to keep him still. The wagons clattered ahead without changing course, and finally drew to a halt at the far end of the pit, where it was easiest to scale the rocky wall. Close to a dozen men clambered down and began to unload lumber, a keg of nails, coils of rope, axes, picks, shovels, and other tools.

Stunned, Will saw that one of the men was his father. Clay Reese, in fact, seemed to be directing the activities of the others. Will also recognized Jess Lacy, proprietor of the Volcano Mercantile, and Harmon Bennett, president of the bank. The other men were laborers.

"First thing to do," Will heard his father say, "is clear a path into the pit so we can take the wagons down there. We'll also have to enlarge the cave opening."

"Dynamite, Clay?" one of the men asked.

"No. Picks and shovels should do it. Then we can start building the ramps and cutting the ice into blocks."

Along with Jess Lacy and Harmon Bennett, Clay

59

Reese disappeared inside the cave. The other men began clearing away rocks, grading a pathway for the wagons.

Will had seen enough. He led the roan away quietly, then mounted and rode out across the plain. His shock had given way to a sense of betrayal.

The town could use ice on these scorching summer days, when cellars weren't able to preserve meat and other perishables; Will understood that. But what he didn't understand was why his father had kept secret his decision to sell the ice. The cave belonged to Will more than to anybody, because he had found it. So why hadn't his father told him about what he intended to do?

Will decided to ask him at dinner.

He rode out to the ranch's north boundary fence to make one of three repairs he had been asked to attend to. By the time he finished, it was too late to make the others; the sun was just starting to wester. He rode on home.

The ranch wagon stood in front of the weathered barn when he arrived, but his father's saddle horse was gone. So were two of the family's three sheep dogs. The other dog followed him into the barn, its barks mingling with the bleating of the sheep in the pens that flanked the shearing shed. He unsaddled his roan, fed it some hay, then crossed to the small sod house under the cottonwoods and went inside.

His mother, in spite of it being the hottest day of the year, was stirring a stew pot on the black iron stove.

She turned, her eyes stern. "Will, where have you been all day?"

"I . . . where's Pa?"

"Out east. A ewe and her lamb got through that fence you were supposed to mend and fell into one of the lava pits. Honestly, Will, I don't know what's the matter with you lately. Your father shouldn't have to attend to your chores."

Clay Reese returned an hour before sundown. Immediately he called Will outside and reprimanded him for neglecting to mend the east fence. "The ewe and her lamb weren't badly hurt," he said, "but they might have been killed."

"I'm sorry, Pa."

His father grunted and started to turn away.

"Pa," Will said, "I was at the ice cave today. I saw you come out with the men from town."

"What? I thought I told you not to go there."

"Yes, sir, you did. But why didn't you tell me you planned to sell the ice?"

"Because it's not your business, that's why."

"Pa, it *is* my business. I found that cave. And we've always talked about things before."

"That's enough!" Clay Reese's lean face was flushed. "We won't discuss it. You stay away from that cave. Understood?"

"Yes, sir."

Baffled and hurt, Will tried to bring the subject up again the next day. But his father once more refused to discuss it. Will went about his chores, a sad, empty feeling growing inside him.

Ever since he'd been small, his father had treated him as an adult. The ranch was not a prosperous one, and all three Reeses worked in partnership to keep it going. Yet now his father was shutting him out, and it hurt; it was making him lose respect for a man he had always looked up to. Will couldn't bear that. He began to think of leaving the ranch, striking out on his own.

He could go to a city—Boise, perhaps—and find work. Then, later on, he could enter college, for his father's thirst for knowledge had been instilled in him, too, and Clay Reese's dream had become his dream. He knew that leaving home would be a form of betrayal, but no more of one than his father's.

He determined to try one more time to talk to the man. It was Saturday noon, and thunderclouds were piling up in the east, when Will approached his father again. Clay Reese was hitching up the wagon for a drive somewhere.

"Pa," he said, "I have to talk to you about the ice cave."

His father's face seemed to cloud as darkly as the sky. "How many times do I have to tell you, Will? There's nothing to discuss. I can't talk now, anyway. I have business to attend to." He climbed into the wagon seat, flicked the reins, and drove off.

Resigned, Will went to his room and packed a bundle. He would leave that night, after his parents were asleep.

• • •

The storm broke around 4 p.m., with thunder and lightning and gusty winds. Clay Reese did not return for supper, and finally Will and his mother ate without him. He had probably decided to wait out the storm in town.

Will spent a restless night as thunder grumbled and rain pelted. It would have been foolish to start his journey in this storm, and, until his father returned, he didn't feel right leaving his mother alone.

Sometime toward morning the storm passed, and he fell into a heavy sleep. It was well past dawn, with the sun blazing again, when his mother awoke him. "Get up, Will," she said. Her voice was anxious. "Your father still isn't home, and I'm worried. You'd best ride into town and try to find him."

"Right away, Ma."

Will dressed quickly, saddled his roan, and rode into the clear, rain-fresh morning. He'd only gone half a mile toward Volcano, however, when he thought of the cave. His father could have gone there yesterday, instead of to town; the ice might have been the business he'd referred to. And it wouldn't take long to check. Will turned his horse off the road and pointed him across open land.

He saw his father's wagon as soon as he came in sight of the lava pit. He sent the roan into a hard run, reined up beside the wagon, and jumped off. There was no sign of Clay Reese, or of any of the laborers, this being Sunday. Will scrambled down the newly graded wagon ramp and ran to the cave opening. It had been enlarged considerably, shored up with timbers. He entered, fumbling in the pocket of his pants for matches.

In the flare of the first match he struck, he saw a jumble of equipment piled to one side; among the axes and picks and coiled rope was a lantern. He used a second match to light the lantern's wick. Now he could see more of the cave—gouges and holes in the once-smooth walls where ice blocks had been cut away; narrow wooden ramps built into the passageway, close to the floor, so that the blocks could be easily dragged out. But there was no sign of his father.

Carrying the lantern, Will hurried deeper into the cave. He went all the way to the solid barrier, then came back and checked some of the smaller chambers. All of them were empty.

He had to fight down panic as he ran back into the main chamber. His father *must* have come into the cave; where could he be? Then Will's gaze picked up the stone steps, the ledge at their top, and the chill air seemed to grow even colder. He climbed the steps, moving as fast as he dared on the slippery surface ice. When he reached the top, he leaned into the fall with the lantern extended.

Down at the bottom of the slide, a huddled form lay alongside the bones of the long-dead animal.

"Pa!" Will shouted the word, shouted it again. But the huddled figure didn't move.

Will half ran, half slid, down the steps and got one

of the coils of rope. Back on the ledge, he found a pro-
jection of rock and tied one end of the rope securely
around it. He played the other end down the fall,
tested the fastening, then swung his body onto the
slide and let himself down to where his father lay.

Clay Reese was unconscious, but still alive. Will's
relief didn't last long, however. Try as he might, he
couldn't revive his father. The man had been here all
night, lying on the ice. He seemed half frozen. If he
did regain consciousness, Will knew, he wouldn't
have the strength to climb out by himself.

Will swiftly tied the rope around his father, under
the arms. When he struggled back up to the ledge, he
tried to pull his father out, but he didn't have the
strength to move the inert figure more than a foot or
so. He had to have help, yet if he left, his father might
die before he could bring men back.

Then another idea came to him, and he wasted no
time putting it into action. He got a second coil of rope
from below, unfastened the first rope from the projec-
tion, and tied the two ropes together to make one long
one. When he took the free end down across the cave
and outside, he had ten feet left.

He climbed to where the roan stood, caught the
bridle, and urged the animal to the cave's entrance. He
tied the rope to the saddle horn, mounted, and backed
the roan until the rope was taut. Then he and the horse
began to pull.

It took agonizing minutes, the roan stumbling a time
or two, almost losing balance. But finally the rope

slackened somewhat, and this told Will his father had at last been drawn to the top of the fall. Dismounting, he raced back into the cave.

Clay Reese lay sprawled across the ledge. He was starting to regain consciousness when Will reached his side.

He managed to get his father to his feet, then down the steps, out of the cave, and to the far end of the pit where the day's heat penetrated. Exhausted, they both sank to the rocky ground. Clay Reese gave his son a weak smile.

"You saved my life," he said when the sun began to take away the chill. "I thought I was a dead man for sure."

"What happened, Pa?"

"I climbed those steps out of curiosity, slipped on the ice, and fell down the slide. I couldn't get back out again." His expression turned rueful. "I told you it could be dangerous in there, Will . . . that you shouldn't go in alone. I should have obeyed my own orders."

"Why did you go in alone?"

"To do some exploring, see if I could tell how big the cave really is. If there's enough ice to last another couple of summers, I reckon we'll start making some money."

"*Start* making money?" Will asked, surprised.

"Will, you have a right to know the truth." His father spoke slowly, the words coming hard for him. "The reason I didn't talk to you about selling the ice is that I was afraid to face up to you. I didn't want anyone to know how close we were to losing the ranch. Until you found the cave, I hadn't been able to make the mortgage payments for some time . . . the bank was getting ready to foreclose."

"So that's why you've been so troubled lately."

"Yes. I worked out an arrangement with Jess Lacy and with Harmon Bennett at the bank. Jess buys the ice at a fair price, and I turn the money over to Mister Bennett. The mortgage will be paid off by next summer. Then we can start saving for your college education."

Will was silent for a time; he felt ashamed at having doubted his father. Finally he said: "Pa, I understand now. But I wish you'd told me all of this before."

"I guess I should have," his father admitted. "But my foolish pride wouldn't let me. I'm sorry, Son."

"I'm sorry, too," Will said. "I . . . well . . . I felt like you didn't need me any more. I was going to leave, go off to Boise and hunt work. I'd be gone now if it hadn't stormed last night."

His father grimaced, his face etched with pain. "This has been a bad misunderstanding, Will. From now on, we'll both be honest with each other. As for the cave, well, we'll explore it together next time. And work together on our ice business, too."

"I'd like that, Pa."

Will stood and began to help his father up the ramp to the wagon. As he did, he glanced over at the mouth of the cave—not his cave, but their cave, the family's cave. Then his eyes met his father's, and they both smiled.

Time of the Wolves

"It was in the time of the wolves that my grandmother came to Kansas." The old woman sat primly on the sofa in her apartment in the senior citizens' complex. Although her faded blue eyes were focused on the window, the historian, who sat opposite her, sensed Mrs. Clark was not seeing the shopping malls and used-car lots that had spilled over into what once was open prairie. As she'd begun speaking, her gaze had turned inward—and into the past.

The historian—who was compiling an oral account of the Kansas pioneers—adjusted the volume button on her tape recorder and looked expectantly at Mrs. Clark. But the descendant of those pioneers was in no hurry; she waited a moment before resuming her story.

"The time of the wolves . . . that's the way I thought of it as a child, and I speak of it that way to this very day. It's fitting . . . those were perilous times, in the Eighteen 'Seventies. Vicious packs of wolves and coyotes roamed . . . fires would sweep the prairie without warning . . . there were disastrous floods . . . and, of course, blizzards. But my grandmother was a true pioneer woman . . . she knew no fear. One time in the winter of Eighteen Seventy-Two. . . ."

Alma Heusser stood in the doorway of the sod house, looking north over the prairie. It was gone four in the afternoon now, and storm clouds were bulking on the horizon. The chill in the air penetrated even her heavy buffalo-skin robe; a hush had fallen, as if all the creatures on the barren plain were holding their breath, waiting for the advent of the snow.

Alma's hand tightened on the rough door frame. Fear coiled in her stomach. Every time John was forced to make the long trek into town she stood like this, awaiting his return. Every moment until his horse appeared in the distance she imagined that some terrible event had taken him from her. And on this night, with the blizzard threatening. . . .

The shadows deepened, purpled by the impending storm. Alma shivered and hugged herself beneath the enveloping robe. The land stretched before her: flat, treeless, its sameness mesmerizing. If she looked at it long enough, her eyes would begin to play tricks on her—tricks that held the power to drive her mad.

She'd heard of a woman who had been driven mad by the prairie: a timid, gentle woman who had traveled some miles east with her husband to gather wood. When they had finally stopped their wagon at a grove, the woman had gotten down and run to a tree—the first tree she had touched in three years. It was said they had had to pry her loose, because she refused to stop hugging it.

The sound of a horse's hoofs came from the distance. Behind Alma, ten-year-old Margaret asked: "Is that him? Is it Papa?"

Alma strained to see through the rapidly gathering

dusk. "No," she said, her voice flat with disappointment. "No, it's only Mister Carstairs."

The Carstairs, William and Sarah, lived on a claim several miles east of there. It was not unusual for William to stop when passing on his way from town. But John had been in town today, too; why had they not ridden back together?

The coil of fear wound tighter as she went to greet him.

"No, I won't dismount," William Carstairs said in response to her invitation to come inside and warm himself. "Sarah doesn't know I am here, so I must be home swiftly. I've come to ask a favor."

"Certainly. What is it?"

"I'm off to the East in the morning. My mother is ill and hasn't much longer . . . she's asked for me. Sarah is anxious about being alone. As you know, she's been homesick these past two years. Will you look after her?"

"Of course." Alma spoke the words with a readiness she did not feel. She did not like Sarah Carstairs. There was something mean-spirited about the young woman, a suspicious air in the way she dealt with others that bordered on the hostile. But looking after neighbors was an inviolate obligation here on the prairie, essential to survival.

"Of course, we'll look after her," she said more warmly, afraid her reluctance had somehow sounded in her voice. "You need not worry."

After William Carstairs had ridden off, Alma remained in the doorway of the sod house until the horizon had receded into darkness. She would wait for John as long as was necessary, hoping that her hunger for the sight of him had the power to bring him home again.

"Neighbors were the greatest treasure my grandparents had," Mrs. Clark explained. "The pioneer people were a warm-hearted lot, open and giving, closer than many of today's families. And the women in particular were a great source of strength and comfort to one another. My grandmother's friendship with Sarah Carstairs, for example. . . ."

"I suppose I must pay a visit to Sarah," Alma said. It was two days later. The snowstorm had never arrived, but, even though it had retreated into Nebraska, another seemed to be on the way. If she didn't go to the Carstairs' claim today, she might not be able to look in on Sarah for some time to come.

John grunted noncommittally and went on trimming the wick of the oil lamp. Alma knew he didn't care for Sarah, either, but he was a taciturn man, slow to voice criticism. And he also understood the necessity of standing by one's neighbors.

"I promised William. He was so worried about her." Alma waited, hoping her husband would forbid her to go because of the impending storm. No such dictum was forthcoming, however. John Heusser was not one to distrust his wife's judgment; he would abide by whatever she decided.

So, driven by a promise she wished she had not been obligated to make, Alma set off on horseback within the hour.

The Carstairs' claim was a poor one, although to Alma's way of thinking it need not be. In the hands of John Heusser it would have been bountiful with wheat and corn, but William Carstairs was an unskilled farmer. His crops had parched even during the past two summers of plentiful rain; his animals fell ill and died of unidentifiable ailments; the house and outbuildings grew ever more ramshackle through his neglect. If Alma were a fanciful woman—and she preferred to believe she was not—she would have said there was a curse on the land. Its appearance on this grim February day did little to dispel the illusion.

In the foreground stood the house, its roof beam sagging, its chimney askew. The barn and other outbuildings behind it looked no better. The horse in the enclosure was bony and spavined; the few chickens seemed too dispirited to scratch at the hard-packed earth. Alma tied her sorrel to the fence and walked toward the house, her reluctance to be there asserting herself until it was nearly a foreboding. There was no sign of welcome from within, none of the flurry of excitement that the arrival of a visitor on the isolated homesteads always occasioned. She called out, knocked at the door. And waited.

After a moment the door opened slowly and Sarah Carstairs looked out. Her dark hair hung loosely about her shoulders; she wore a muslin dress dyed the rich brown of walnut bark. Her eyes were deeply circled— haunted, Alma thought.

Quickly she shook off the notion and smiled. "We've heard that Mister Carstairs had to journey East," she said. "I thought you might enjoy some company."

The younger woman nodded. Then she opened the door wider and motioned Alma inside.

The room was much like Alma's main room at home, with narrow, tall windows, a rough board floor, and an iron stove for both cooking and heating. The curtains at the windows were plain burlap grain sacks, not at all like Alma's neatly stitched muslin ones, with their appliqués of flowers. The furnishings—a pair of rockers, pine cabinet, sideboard, and table—had been new when the Carstairs arrived from the East two years before, but their surfaces were coated with the grime that accumulated from cooking.

Sarah shut the door and turned to face Alma, still not speaking. To cover her confusion Alma thrust out the cornbread she had brought. The younger woman took it, nodding thanks. After a slight hesitation, she set it on the table and motioned somewhat gracelessly at one of the rockers. "Please," she said.

Alma undid the fastenings of her heavy cloak and sat down, puzzled by the strange reception. Sarah went to the stove and added a log, in spite of the room already being quite warm.

"He sent you to spy on me, didn't he?"

The words caught Alma by complete surprise. She

stared at Sarah's narrow back, unable to make a reply.

Sarah turned, her sharp features pinched by what might have been anger. "That is why you're here, is it not?" she asked.

"Mister Carstairs did ask us to look out for you in his absence, yes."

"How like him," Sarah said bitterly.

Alma could think of nothing to say to that.

Sarah offered her coffee. As she prepared it, Alma studied the young woman. In spite of the heat in the room and her proximity to the stove, she rubbed her hands together; her shawl slipped off her thin shoulders, and she quickly pulled it back. When the coffee was ready—a bitter, nearly unpalatable brew—she sat cradling the cup in her hands, as if to draw even more warmth from it.

After her earlier strangeness Sarah seemed determined to talk about the commonplace: the storm that was surely due, the difficulty of obtaining proper cloth, her hope that William would not forget the bolt of calico she had requested he bring. She asked Alma about making soap. Had she ever done so? Would she allow her to help the next time so she might learn? As they spoke, she began to wipe beads of moisture from her brow. The room remained very warm; Alma removed her cloak and draped it over the back of the rocker.

Outside, the wind was rising, and the light that came through the narrow windows was tinged with gray. Alma became impatient to be off for home before the storm arrived, but she also became concerned with leaving Sarah alone. The young woman's conversation was rapidly growing erratic and rambling; she broke off in the middle of sentences to laugh irrelevantly. Her brow continued moist, and she threw off her shawl, fanning herself. Alma, who like all frontier women had had considerable experience at doctoring the sick, realized Sarah had been taken by a fever.

Her first thought was to take Sarah to her own home, where she might look after her properly, but one glance out the window discouraged her. The storm was nearing quickly now; the wind gusted, tearing at the dried cornstalks in William Carstairs's uncleared fields, and the sky was streaked with black and purple. A ride of several miles in such weather would be the death of Sarah, do Alma no good, either. She was here for the duration, with only a sick woman to help her make the place secure.

She glanced at Sarah, but the other woman seemed unaware of what was going on outside. Alma said: "You're feeling poorly, aren't you?"

Sarah shook her head vehemently. A strand of dark brown hair fell across her forehead and clung there damply. Alma sensed she was not a woman who would give in easily to illness, would fight any suggestion that she take to her bed until she was near collapse. She thought over the remedies she had administered to others in such a condition, wondered whether Sarah's supplies included the necessary sassafras tea or quinine.

Sarah was rambling again—about the prairie, its loneliness and desolation. ". . . listen to that wind! It's with us every moment. I hate the wind and the cold, I hate the nights when the wolves prowl. . . ."

A stealthy touch of cold moved along Alma's spine. She, too, feared the wolves and coyotes. John told her it came from having Germanic blood. Their older relatives had often spoken in hushed tones of the wolf packs in the Black Forest. Many of their native fairy tales and legends concerned the cruel cunning of the animals, but John was always quick to point out that these were only stories. "Wolves will not attack a human unless they sense sickness or weakness," he often asserted. "You need only take caution."

But all of the settlers, John included, took great precautions against the roaming wolf packs; no one went out onto the prairie unarmed. And the stories of merciless and unprovoked attacks could not all be unfounded. . . .

"I hear wolves at night," Sarah said. "They scratch on the door and the sod. They're hungry. Oh, yes, they're hungry."

Alma suddenly got to her feet, unable to sit for the tautness in her limbs. She felt Sarah's eyes on her as she went to the sideboard and lit the oil lamp. When she turned to Sarah again, the young woman had tilted her head against the high back of the rocker and was viewing her through slitted lids. There was a glitter in the dark crescents that remained visible that struck Alma as somehow malicious.

"Are you afraid of the wolves, Alma?" she asked slyly.

"Anyone with good sense is."

"And you in particular?"

"Of course, I'd be afraid if I met one face-to-face!"

"Only if you were face-to-face with it? Then you won't be afraid staying here with me when they scratch at the door. I tell you, I hear them every night. Their claws go *snick, snick* on the boards. . . ."

The words were baiting. Alma felt her dislike for Sarah Carstairs gather strength. She said calmly: "Then you've noticed the storm is fast approaching."

Sarah extended a limp arm toward the window. "Look at the snow."

Alma glanced over there, saw the first flakes drifting past the wavery pane of glass. The sense of foreboding she'd felt upon her arrival intensified, sending little prickles over the surface of her skin.

Firmly she reined in her fear and met Sarah's eyes with a steady gaze. "You're right . . . I must stay here. I'll be as little trouble to you as possible."

"Why should you be trouble? I'll be glad of your company." Her tone mocked the meaning of the words. "We can talk. It's a long time since I've had anyone to talk to. We'll talk of my William."

Alma glanced at the window again, anxious to put her horse into the barn, out of the snow. She thought of the revolver she carried in her saddlebag as defense against the dangers of the prairie; she would feel safer if she brought it inside with her.

"We'll talk of my William," Sarah repeated "You'd like that, wouldn't you, Alma?"

"Of course. But first I must tend to my horse."

"Yes, of course, you'd like talking of William. You like talking to him. All those times when he stops at your place on his way home to me. On his way home, when your John isn't there. Oh, yes, Alma, I know about those visits." Sarah's eyes were wide now, the malicious light shining brightly.

Alma caught her breath. She opened her mouth to contradict the words, then shut it. It was the fever talking, she told herself, exaggerating the fears and delusions that life on the frontier could sometimes foster. There was no sense trying to reason with Sarah. What mattered now was to put the horse up and fetch her weapon. She said briskly—"We'll discuss this when I've returned."—donned her cloak, and stepped out into the storm.

The snow was sheeting along on a northwesterly gale. The flakes were small and hard; they stung her face like hailstones. The wind made it difficult to walk; she leaned into it, moving slowly toward the hazy outline of her sorrel. He stood by the rail, his hoofs moving skittishly. Alma grasped his halter, clung to it a moment before she began leading him toward the ramshackle barn. The chickens had long ago fled to their coop. Sarah's bony bay was nowhere in sight.

The doors to the barn stood open, the interior in darkness. Alma led the sorrel inside and waited until her eyes accustomed themselves to the gloom. When they had, she spied a lantern hanging next to the door, matches and flint nearby. She fumbled with them, got the lantern lit, and looked around.

Sarah's bay stood in one of the stalls, apparently accustomed to looking out for itself. The stall was dirty, and the entire barn held an air of neglect. She set the lantern down, unsaddled the sorrel, and fed and watered both horses. As she turned to leave, she saw the dull gleam of an axe lying on top of a pile of wood. Without considering why she was doing so, she picked it up and carried it, along with her gun, outside. The barn doors were warped and difficult to secure, but with some effort she managed.

Back in the house, she found Sarah's rocker empty. She set down the axe and the gun, calling out in alarm. A moan came from beyond the rough burlap that curtained off the next room. Alma went over and pushed aside the cloth.

Sarah lay on a brass bed, her hair fanned out on the pillows. She had crawled under the tumbled quilts and blankets. Alma approached and put a hand to her forehead; it was hot, but Sarah was shivering.

Sarah moaned again. Her eyes opened and focused unsteadily on Alma. "Cold," she said. "So cold. . . ."

"You've taken a fever." Alma spoke briskly, a manner she'd found effective with sick people. "Did you remove your shoes before getting into bed?"

Sarah nodded.

"Good. It's best you keep your clothes on, though . . .

this storm is going to be a bad one . . . you'll need them for warmth."

Sarah rolled onto her side and drew herself into a ball, shivering violently. She mumbled something, but her words were muffled.

Alma leaned closer. "What did you say?"

"The wolves . . . they'll come tonight, scratching. . . ."

"No wolves are going to come here in this storm. Anyway, I've a gun and the axe from your woodpile. No harm will come to us. Try to rest now, perhaps sleep. When you wake, I'll bring some tea that will help break the fever."

Alma went toward the door, then turned to look back at the sick woman. Sarah was curled on her side, but she had moved her head and was watching her. Her eyes were slitted once more, and the light from the lamp in the next room gleamed off them—hard and cold as the icicles that must be forming on the eaves.

Alma was seized by an unreasoning chill. She moved through the door, out into the lamplight, toward the stove's warmth. As she busied herself with finding things in the cabinet, she felt a violent tug of home.

Ridiculous to fret, she told herself. John and Margaret would be fine. They would worry about her, of course, but would know she had arrived here well in advance of the storm. And they would also credit her with the good sense not to start back home on such a night.

She rummaged through the shelves and drawers, found the herbs and tea and some roots that would make a healing brew. Outside, there was a momentary quieting of the wind; in the bedroom Sarah, also, lay quiet. Alma put on the kettle and sat down to wait for it to boil.

It was then that she heard the first wolf howls, not far away on the prairie.

"The bravery of the pioneer women has never been equaled," Mrs. Clark told the historian. "And there was a solidarity, a sisterhood among them that you don't see any more. That sisterhood was what sustained my grandmother and Sarah Carstairs as they battled the wolves. . . ."

For hours the wolves howled in the distance. Sarah awoke, throwing off the covers, complaining of the heat. Alma dosed her repeatedly with the herbal brew and waited for the fever to break. Sarah tossed about on the bed, raving about wolves and the wind and William. She seemed to have some fevered notion that her husband had deserted her, and nothing Alma would say would calm her. Finally she wore herself out and slipped into a troubled sleep.

Alma prepared herself some tea and pulled one of the rockers close to the stove. She was bone-tired, and the cold was bitter now, invading the little house through every crack and pore in the sod. Briefly she thought she should bring Sarah into the main room, prepare a pallet on the floor nearer the heat source, but she decided it would do the woman more harm than good to be moved. As she sat warming herself and sipping the tea, she gradually became aware of an eerie hush and realized the wind had ceased.

Quickly she set down her cup and went to the window. The snow had stopped, too. Like its sister storm of two days before, this one had retreated north, leaving behind a barren white landscape. The moon had appeared, near to full, and its stark light glistened off the snow.

And against the snow moved the black silhouettes of the wolves.

They came from the north, rangy and shaggy, more like ragged shadows than flesh and blood creatures. Their howling was silenced now, and their gait held purpose. Alma counted five of them, all of a good size yet bony. Hungry.

She stepped back from the window and leaned against the wall beside it. Her breathing was shallow, and she felt strangely light-headed. For a moment she stood, one hand pressed to her midriff, bringing her senses under control. Then she moved across the room, to where William Carstairs's Winchester rifle hung on the wall. When she had it in her hands, she stood looking resolutely at it.

Of course, Alma knew how to fire a rifle; all frontier women did. But she was only a fair shot with it, a far better shot with her revolver. She could use a rifle to fire at the wolves at a distance, but the best she could hope for was to frighten them. Better to wait and see what transpired.

She set the rifle down and turned back to the window. The wolves were still some distance away. And what if they did come to the house, scratch at the door as Sarah had claimed? The house was well built; there was little harm the wolves could do it.

Alma went to the door to the bedroom. Sarah still slept, the covers pushed down from her shoulders. Alma went in and pulled them up again. Then she returned to the main room and the rocker.

The first scratchings came only minutes later. *Snick, snick* on the boards, just as Sarah had said.

Alma gripped the arms of the rocker with icy fingers. The revolver lay in her lap.

The scratching went on. Snuffling noises, too. In the bedroom, Sarah cried out in protest. Alma got up and looked in on her. The sick woman was writhing on the bed. "They're out there! I know they are!"

Alma went to her. "Hush, they won't hurt us." She tried to rearrange Sarah's covers, but she only thrashed harder.

"They'll break the door, they'll find a way in, they'll. . . ."

Alma pressed her hand over Sarah's mouth. "Stop it! You'll only do yourself harm."

Surprisingly Sarah calmed. Alma wiped sweat from her brow and waited. The young woman continued to lie quietly.

When Alma went back to the window, she saw that

the wolves had retreated. They stood together, several yards away, as if discussing how to breech the house.

Within minutes they returned. Their scratchings became bolder now, their claws ripped and tore at the sod. Heavy bodies thudded against the door, making the boards tremble.

In the bedroom, Sarah cried out. This time Alma ignored her.

The onslaught became more intense. Alma checked the load on William Carstairs's rifle, then looked at her pistol. Five rounds left. Five rounds, five wolves. . . .

The wolves were in a frenzy now—incited, perhaps, by the odor of sickness within the house. Alma remembered John's words: "They will not attack a human unless they sense sickness or weakness." There was plenty of both here.

One of the wolves leapt at the window. The thick glass creaked but did not shatter. There were more thumps at the door; its boards groaned.

Alma took her pistol in both hands, held it ready, moved toward the door.

In the bedroom, Sarah cried out for William. Once again Alma ignored her.

The coil of fear that was so often in the pit of Alma's stomach wound taut. Strangely it gave her strength. She trained the revolver's muzzle on the door, ready should it give.

The attack came from a different quarter: The window shattered, glass smashing on the floor. A gray head appeared, tried to wiggle through the narrow casement. Alma smelled its foul odor, saw its fangs. She fired once . . . twice.

The wolf dropped out of sight.

The assault on the door ceased. Cautiously Alma moved forward. When she looked out the window, she saw the wolf lying dead on the ground—and the others renewing their attack on the door.

Alma scrambled back as another shaggy gray head appeared in the window frame. She fired. The wolf dropped back, snarling.

It lunged once more. Her finger squeezed the trigger. The wolf fell.

One round left. Alma turned, meaning to fetch the rifle. But Sarah stood behind her.

The sick woman wavered on her feet. Her face was coated with sweat, her hair tangled. In her hands she held the axe that Alma had brought from the woodpile.

In the instant before Sarah raised it above her head, Alma saw her eyes. They were made wild by something more than fever. The woman was totally mad.

Disbelief made Alma slow. It was only as the blade began its descent that she was able to move aside.

The blade came down, whacked into the boards where she had stood.

Her sudden motion nearly put her on the floor. She stumbled, fought to steady herself.

From behind her came a scrambling sound. She whirled, saw a wolf wriggling halfway through the window casement.

Sarah was struggling to lift the axe.

Alma pivoted and put her last bullet into the wolf's head.

Sarah had raised the axe. Alma dropped the revolver and rushed at her. She slammed into the young woman's shoulder, sent her spinning toward the stove. The axe crashed to the floor.

As she fell against the hot metal Sarah screamed—a sound more terrifying than the howls of the wolves.

"My grandmother was made of stronger cloth than Sarah Carstairs," Mrs. Clark said. "The wolf attack did irreparable damage to poor Sarah's mind. She was never the same again."

Alma was never sure what had driven the two remaining wolves off—whether it was the death of the others or the terrible keening of the sick and injured woman in the sod house. She was never clear on how she managed to do what needed to be done for Sarah, nor how she got through the remainder of that terrible night. But in the morning when John arrived—so afraid for her safety that he had left Margaret at home and braved the drifted snow alone—Sarah was bandaged and put to bed. The fever had broken, and they were able to transport her to their own home after securing the battered house against the elements.

If John sensed that something more terrible than a wolf attack had transpired during those dark hours, he never spoke of it. Certainly he knew Sarah was in grave trouble, though, because she never said a word throughout her entire convalescence, save to give her thanks when William returned—summoned by them from the East—and took her home. Within the month the Carstairs had deserted their claim and left Kansas, to return to their native state of Vermont. There, Alma hoped, the young woman would somehow find peace.

As for herself, fear still curled in the pit of her stomach as she waited for John on those nights when he was away. But no longer was she shamed by the feeling. The fear, she knew now, was a friend—something that had stood her in good stead once, would be there should she again need it. And now, when she crossed the prairie, she did so with courage, for she and the lifesaving fear were one.

Her story done, Mrs. Clark smiled at the historian. "As I've said, my dear," she concluded, "the women of the Kansas frontier were uncommon in their valor. They faced dangers we can barely imagine today. And they were fearless, one and all."

Her eyes moved away to the window, and to the housing tracts and shoddy commercial enterprises beyond it. "I can't help wondering how women like Alma Heusser would feel about the way the prairie looks today," she added. "I should think they would hate it, and yet. . . ."

The historian had been about to shut off her recorder, but now she paused for a final comment. "And yet?" she prompted.

"And yet I think that somehow my grandmother would have understood that our world isn't as bad as it appears on the surface. Alma Heusser has always struck me as a woman who knew that things aren't always as they seem."

Sisters

The first time Lydia Whitesides saw Curious Cat looking through her kitchen window, she was more startled than frightened. She was sifting flour preparatory to making the day's bread, and had turned to see where she'd set her big wooden spoon when a face appeared above the sill. It was deeply tanned, framed by shiny black braids. The dark eyes regarded Lydia solemnly for a moment, and then the face disappeared.

Well, that's quite something, she thought. The Indians in this part of central Kansas were well known for their curiosity about the white man's ways, and Lydia had heard tell of squaws and braves who would enter settlers' homes unbidden and snoop about, but none had ever paid the Whitesides a visit. Until now.

"Thank the Lord it was a timid squaw," she murmured, and went on with her baking.

Lydia was not unfamiliar with Indians. She and her husband, Ben, operated a general store on the main street of Salina, and, when she clerked there in the afternoons, she traded bolts of cloth, sacks of flour and sugar, and dried fruit—but never firearms or whiskey; the Whitesides stood firm on that point—for the pelts and furs that the Kaw tribesmen brought in. The members of this friendly tribe spent hours examining the many wares, and the women in particular displayed a fascination with white babies. Their demeanor, however, was restrained, and previously

Lydia had seen no evidence of the Indians' legendary boldness.

In the remaining few days of that month of April, 1866, the squaw's face appeared frequently at the kitchen window. At first she would merely stare at Lydia, then her gaze became more lively, moving about the room, stopping here and there at objects of interest. Lydia watched and waited, in much the same way she would were she attempting to tame a bird or squirrel. Finally, a week after her initial visit, the woman climbed up on the sill and dropped lightly to the kitchen floor. Lydia smiled, but made no move that would frighten her.

The squaw returned the smile tentatively and glanced about. Then she went to the nearby stove and put out a hand to touch it. Its black iron was hot, and the woman quickly drew back her hand. She regarded the stove for a moment, then went on to the dish cupboard, drawing aside its curtain and examining the crockery. As she proceeded through the room, looking into drawers and cupboards, she barely acknowledged Lydia's presence. After some ten minutes of this, she climbed through the window and was gone.

Curious, Lydia thought, like a cat. And at that moment, in her mind, Curious Cat was named.

The next day Curious Cat returned and reëxamined the kitchen. The day after that she moved boldly through the rest of the house. Lydia followed, not attempting to stop her. She had heard from other settlers that an Indian intent on snooping could not be reasoned with; to them, their behavior was not rude and intrusive, but merely friendly. Besides, Lydia was as interested in the squaw as the squaw was in the house.

Curious Cat seemed fascinated by the mantel clock; she stood before it, her head swaying, as if mesmerized by its ticking. The spinning wheel likewise enchanted her; she touched the wheel and, when it moved, pulled her hand away in surprise. She gazed for a long moment at the bed with its patchwork quilt and lace pillow covers. When she turned her eyes to Lydia, they were clouded by bewilderment. Lydia placed her hands together and tilted her head against them, her eyes closed. Curious Cat nodded, the universal symbol for sleep having explained all. Before she left that morning she placed her hand on Lydia's stomach, rounded in her fourth month of pregnancy.

"You papoose?" she asked.

"Yes. Papoose in five moons."

Curious Cat beamed with pleasure and departed her usual way.

Thus began the friendship between the two women— so different that they could barely converse. Lydia did not mention Curious Cat's morning visits to her husband. Ben had spent a year in Dodge City before he had met Lydia and settled in Salina. He had arrived there in 1864, shortly after the government massacre of the Cheyennes at Sand Creek, Colorado and had seen the dreadful Indian retaliation against the plains settlers. Murder, plundering, and destruction had been the fruits of the white man's arrogance, and on the frontier no settler was safe.

Although Ben was fully aware of the differences between the peaceable Kaws and the hostile Comanches, Cheyennes, Arapahoes, and Kiowas, he had been badly scarred by his frontier experiences—so much so that he preferred Lydia or his hired clerk to wait on the Indians who came to the store. He would have been most alarmed had he known that a Kaw woman regularly visited his pregnant wife at home. Although Lydia was not afraid of her husband's anger, she held her tongue about the squaw. After all, she did not wish Ben to be troubled, nor did she intend to bar the door—or, in this case, the window—to Curious Cat.

During her afternoons at the store, Lydia made discreet inquiries about Curious Cat among the squaws whose English she knew to be better than average. The woman was easy to describe because of an odd buffalo horn necklace she habitually wore. When Lydia did so, the women exchanged glances that she could only interpret as disapproving.

Finally a tall, raw-boned woman who seemed to be the leader of the group spoke scornfully. "That one. Cheyenne squaw of White Tail."

That explained the disapproving looks. White Tail was a local chieftain who at times in the past had allied himself with the hostile tribes to the west. That he had taken a Cheyenne wife had further proven his renegade leanings to his people. Curious Cat undoubtedly lived a lonely existence among the Kaws—as lonely, for sure, as that which Lydia herself lived among the ladies of Salina.

It was not that the townswomen shunned her. If anything, they were exceptionally polite in their dealings, particularly when they came to trade at the Whitesides' store. But between them and Lydia there was a distance as tangible as the pane of glass that would stand between her and Curious Cat should she close the window to her. The townswomen did not mean to ostracize or hurt Lydia; they simply had no way of engaging in social intercourse with one of her background.

She had been born nearly eighteen years before to parents who traveled with a medicine show—one of the first small rag-tag bands to roam the frontier, hawking their nostrums to the settlers. Her parents had performed a magic act—The Sultan and Princess Fatima—and Lydia's earliest recollections were of the swaying motion of the wagons as they moved from outpost to outpost. Even now she could close her eyes and easily conjure up the creak of their wheels, the murmur and roar of the crowds. She could see the flickering of torchlight on the canvas tent. And she could smell the sweat and grease-paint and kerosene and—after her mother died when she was only five—the whiskey.

After his wife's death, her father had taken to drink, and to gambling. After the shows he went to the saloons in the strange towns, looking for a game of faro. Often he took his young daughter with him. Lydia learned to sleep on his lap, under poker tables, anywhere—oblivious to the talk and occasional shouts and tinny piano music that went on around her. When she was nine, he put her to work as Princess Fatima. She hated the whistles and catcalls and often-evil attention from the men in the crowd. Many was the time that she stumbled with weariness. But in her world one did what one had to, even a nine-year-old. And she was effective as Princess Fatima. She knew that.

Ben Whitesides had realized it, too, the first time he saw her in Wichita, where he had drifted after leaving Dodge City. But, as he confided to her later, he had seen more than her prettiness and easy charm, had seen the goodness she hid deep inside her. In spite of the unwholesome reputation of the show people, he had courted her. For three weeks he had followed the caravan as it made its way from Wichita to Montgomery County; at night his clean, shining face would be the first she would spy in the crowd. Lydia had her doubts about this gentle, soft-spoken young man—his fascination with her, she thought, bespoke a lack of good sense. And much as she hated her nomadic existence, it was all she had known. Much as her increasingly besotted father angered her, she loved him. But Ben persisted, and in one month more he made her his wife.

Ben Whitesides had given her a home, a respectable

livelihood, the promise of a child. But he could not eradicate the loneliness of her life here in Salina. No one had been able to do that. Until now. Now there were the eagerly awaited visits from the Indian woman she had named Curious Cat.

At first the two could converse very little. Curious Cat knew some English—as most of the members of the local tribe did—but she seemed reluctant to speak it. Lydia knew a few Indian words, so one day she gave Curious Cat a piece of fresh-baked cornbread and said the word for it in Kaw. She was rewarded by an immediate softening in the other woman's eyes. The next day Curious Cat pointed questioningly at the stove. Lydia named it in English. Curious Cat repeated the word. Their mutual language lessons had begun.

In the weeks that followed, Curious Cat learned the English for every object in the house. Lydia learned words, too—whether they were Kaw or Cheyenne she wasn't certain. Curious Cat told her her name—Silent Bird—and Lydia called her by it, but since the woman was neither bird-like nor silent, she remained Curious Cat in Lydia's mind. In a short time she and her Indian friend were able to communicate simple thoughts and stories, to give one another some idea of their lives before the day Curious Cat had decided to look into the white woman's world through Lydia's kitchen window.

The first of these exchanges came about on the day after Lydia's birthday, when she wore for the first time a soapstone brooch etched with the shape of a graceful, leafless tree—her gift from Ben. The tree, her husband said, reminded him of those he had seen on the far western plains, before fortune had brought him to her.

Curious Cat noticed the brooch immediately upon her arrival. She approached Lydia and fingered it hesitantly. The intensity of emotion in her liquid brown eyes startled Lydia; the squaw seldom betrayed her feelings. Now she seemed in pain, as if the brooch called forth some unwanted memory.

After a moment she moved away and went to see what Lydia was baking—her ritual upon arriving. Her movements were listless, however, her curiosity about what was in the oven obviously forced. Lydia motioned for her to come into the parlor and sit beside her on the settee. Curious Cat did so, placing her hands together in the lap of her faded calico skirt.

Lydia touched the brooch with her forefinger. "What is it? What is wrong?"

Curious Cat looked away, feigning interest in the spinning wheel.

"No, you must tell me."

The anguished brown eyes returned to Lydia's. "The tree . . . my home. . . ."

"The tree reminds you of where you were born, on the plains?"

Hesitation. Then a nod.

"Tell me about it."

Curious Cat's face became a battleground where emotions warred: sadness, yearning, and anger. For a moment Lydia feared that what she wanted to say would be too much for their shared rudimentary language, but then Curious Cat began to tell her story in a patchwork of broken phrases, gestures, and facial expressions that conveyed far more than the most eloquent speech.

She had been born on the far western reaches of the Great Plains, to a chieftain of one of the Cheyenne's most powerful clans. When she reached womanhood, a match had been arranged with the son of another powerful chieftain—a union that would ally the two great clans. The young man, Curious Cat indicated, was far more than agreeable. She had watched him from afar, and found him brave as well as handsome.

But then came the massacre of the Cheyennes at Sand Creek. Curious Cat's father was killed, and her brother disappeared after subsequent hostilities near Wichita. It was said among his tribesmen that he had fled, a coward. Now Curious Cat and her mother found themselves ostracized as family of a traitor, with no man to protect and provide for them. The young brave to whom Curious Cat had been promised would no longer look upon her face.

Within months, Curious Cat's mother had died, broken and weakened by the struggle to survive. Curious Cat lived off the meager kindnesses people showed her. When White Tail of the Kaws traveled west, hoping to strike an alliance between his tribe and the war-like Cheyennes, his eye was caught by the ragged outcast; he spoke of his interest to the chief of her clan, and it was deemed suitable that she leave as White Tail's squaw. With her departure, a shameful reminder would be removed.

Now, Curious Cat told Lydia, she lived among the Kaws much as she had among her own people. True, she had White Tail to protect her, and life was not such a struggle. But his war-like ways had made him and his family suspect, and the women kept their distance from his squaw. She was to be forever a stranger in the Kaw village.

So this, Lydia thought when Curious Cat was still, was the root of the bond she had sensed between them. They were both strangers condemned to loneliness. After a moment she told her own story to the Cheyenne woman, and, when she was finished, they sat silently, yet at ease. The bond between them was welded strong.

The trouble began when customers at the store told Ben they had seen a squaw entering and leaving his property on a number of occasions. Ben was concerned and questioned Lydia about it. She readily admitted as much.

"The Kaw are a curious people, Ben. The squaw comes to spy. But she is harmless."

"She may very well be, but what of her tribesmen?"

"No one has come here but her."

"Still . . . they say she is a strange one. An outcast."

"And how do they know this is the woman of whom they speak?"

"The buffalo horn necklace she wears makes her recognizable. It is Cheyenne, and they *are* war-like."

Lydia pictured the necklace, which Curious Cat fingered often, as if to preserve her last link to the people who had sent her into exile. "But if she is with the Kaws, she is Cheyenne no longer."

"You cannot be sure of that. The Indians are a peculiar race . . . who knows what they may be thinking, or where their loyalties lie?"

Lydia was quite sure that Curious Cat's loyalties lay with no tribe, but she knew she could not explain that to Ben. She fell silent, seeking a way out of the dilemma.

Ben said: "I am only thinking of you and our child. The next time this squaw comes around, you must bar the door."

The way out was in his words. "That I will," she agreed. Ben was unaware that Curious Cat had entered and left by the window. By saying she would bar the door, she was not actually lying to her husband.

As spring turned to summer, Lydia continued to enjoy the Indian woman's companionship. Curious Cat came most mornings, cautiously so as not to come to the further attention of the townspeople. Together they baked bread, and Lydia demonstrated the uses of the spinning wheel, which was still an object of fascination for the squaw. They conversed with greater ease, and sometimes Curious Cat would sing songs with strange words and odd melodies that somehow conveyed their meaning. Lydia reciprocated with the lullabies that she would soon sing to her child. The child quickened within her, and the days passed swiftly.

The weather turned hot and arid. No breeze cooled the flat land. From the west the news was bad: prairie fires swept out of control near Wilson and Lincoln; a sudden fierce gale had caused fire to jump the Saline River and destroy the tiny settlement of Greenport. The Indians were on the rampage again, too. Enraged by the wholesale slaughter of buffalo, the Cheyennes and Comanches attacked railroad crews and frontier settlements, plundering and murdering. Nearby Mitchell County was in a constant state of siege, and the people of Salina began to fear that the raids would soon extend east to their own territory. Of the prairie fires Lydia and Curious Cat spoke often. About the Indian raids they remained silent.

As the news from the beleaguered settlements worsened, the populace of Salina grew fearful. The Kaws, always welcomed before, were looked at askance when they came to trade at the Whitesides' store. Peaceable merchants such as Ben, who seldom handled guns, armed themselves. Women kept doors locked and rifles close to hand. The heat intensified the undercurrent of panic. Tempers grew raw; brawls and shootings in the saloons increased. During the first week in August the distant glow of prairie fire intruded on slumber.

Ben Whitesides took to returning home for his

midday meal to reassure himself of Lydia's safety now that the days of her confinement approached and she was no longer able to come to the store. She was agreeable to the arrangement, but it meant taking care that Curious Cat departed before the time Ben customarily arrived. On a stifling day in mid-August, however, she let awareness of the hour slip away from her. She and Curious Cat were taking cornbread from the oven when Ben came through the kitchen door.

Ben saw the squaw immediately. He stopped, suddenly pale, his hand on the doorknob. Curious Cat seemed frozen. Lydia herself could not move or breathe. The sweat that beaded her forehead and upper lip felt oddly cold. The hush was so great that she could hear the mantel clock ticking in the parlor.

Ben's eyes were jumpy, wild. Lydia knew he did not comprehend that he had walked in on a peaceable scene. She put out a hand to him, opened her mouth to explain.

The motion freed Curious Cat; she slipped over toward the window. Ben's glazed eyes jerked after her, and his hand moved under his coat, to where he had taken to carrying his pistol.

Curious Cat gave a guttural cry and began scrambling onto the sill. Lydia's gaze was transfixed as Ben took out the gun. Then she heard a tearing sound and whirled. Curious Cat's skirt was caught on a nail, and she was struggling to free it. Lydia swung back toward Ben. He was leveling the pistol at the squaw.

"No, Ben!" she cried.

He paid her no mind.

"No!" Lydia flung herself at him.

Ben jerked the gun up. A shot boomed, deafeningly. The room seemed to shake, and plaster showered down from the ceiling.

Lydia crumpled to the floor, and cowered there, her ears ringing. The plaster continued to rain down, stinging the skin of her arms and face. When she looked up, she saw Ben standing over her. He was staring at the gun, his whole body shaking.

"Dear God," he said in a choked voice. "Dear God, what I might have done!"

Lydia turned her head toward the window. Curious Cat had gone.

After that day Curious Cat came no more, and a silence descended upon the Whitesides' home. A familiar but unaccustomed silence during the days as Lydia went about her household tasks alone. An unnatural silence at night, between herself and Ben.

Once his shock had abated, Ben had become angry and remained angry for days. When the anger faded, he was left with a deep sense of betrayal at Lydia's months-long deception, a hurt that shone in his eyes every time he looked at her. Lydia's pain was twofold: by lying to Ben she had put a distance between them just before the birth of their child, when they should have been drawing closer than ever. And she had exposed Curious Cat, her only friend, to danger and humiliation.

During the stifling late-summer nights she lay huge and restless in the double bed, listening to Ben's deep breathing and thinking of how she had wronged him. Then her thoughts would turn to Curious Cat, and she would wonder how her friend was faring. She feared that, like Ben, the squaw thought she had betrayed her, somehow held her responsible for the near shooting. But mostly she pictured Curious Cat as lonely, exiled once again to her life among the unaccepting Kaws.

Even the now-strong movements of her unborn child failed to cheer Lydia. She felt incapable of facing the momentous event ahead. Not the birth itself, that was painful and dangerous, but physical ordeals had never daunted her. What she feared was that she might not be wise enough to guide the small and helpless life that would soon be placed in her hands. After all, if she had so wronged her husband and her only friend, how could she expect to do the right things for her child?

On a brilliant September morning Curious Cat came again. She slipped through the kitchen window and dropped to the floor as Lydia was shelling a bushel of peas. When she saw her Indian friend, Lydia felt her face flush with delight. But Curious Cat did not smile. She did not check the baking bread or peer into the larder. Instead, she stared at Lydia, her face intense.

"What is it?" Lydia asked, starting to rise.

Curious Cat came to her, placed her hands on her shoulders, and pushed her gently into the chair. She squatted on the floor in front of her, eyes burning with determination.

"You help," she said.

"Help? Yes, of course. What . . . ?"

"You tell. Save people."

"Tell what? Who?"

Curious Cat's gaze wavered. For a moment Lydia thought she might run off. Then she said: "Cheyenne. Many. Come White Tail, talk war."

"War? Where?"

"Now near Shady Bend. Be here two sleeps."

Shady Bend was in Lincoln County, on the other side of the Saline River. Two sleeps—two days—was what it would take a war party, traveling fast, to reach Salina. "They plan to attack *here?*"

Curious Cat nodded.

"Will White Tail join them?"

She shook her head in the negative. "White Tail grows old. Tired of war. I come to tell you make ready. Save people."

"Why are you telling me? The Cheyennes are *your* people. They will be slaughtered."

Curious Cat fingered her buffalo horn necklace. Then she rose and was gone through the window.

At first Ben was skeptical of what Lydia told him.

"Why would this squaw betray her own people in order to save our town?" he asked. "I fear this is a false story . . . some sort of retaliation for my nearly shooting her."

"I think not. Curious Cat was badly used by the Cheyennes . . . her loyalty is no longer with them. She is Kaw now, and her husband White Tail wants no part of this war."

Ben was watching Lydia's face, frowning. "How do you know so much about the squaw?"

"She told me."

"How could she tell you? Indians can barely speak English. And surely you cannot speak Kaw or Cheyenne."

"Curious Cat speaks English well, and I know a fair amount of her language as well. We taught one another, and we used to talk often."

Ben's face darkened. He did not like to be reminded of how the squaw had visited his house. "Perhaps you talked, but not of such important things as those. Of baking and spinning, yes. But of the squaw's loyalty to her people, or White Tail's feelings about a Cheyenne war? I think not."

Lydia felt her anger rise at his patronizing dismissal. "One does not need important-sounding words to discuss important things, Ben."

"I am only saying that it seems improbable. . . ."

"Curious Cat and I may share a limited language, but we talked about anything we wished. And we did not hide our feelings within a cloak of silence."

Her husband looked as if he were about to make a sharp retort. Then he bit his lip, obviously understanding her reference to his recent silence. After a moment he said: "Do you really believe the squaw is telling the truth?"

"I do."

"And you are certain her loyalty no longer lies with the Cheyennes?"

"Nor with the Kaws. She feels alone in the world."

Lydia could see that Ben did not want to believe her, did not want to give up his conviction that all Indians were devious and sly. But he was a reasonable man, and, after thinking for a moment, he shook his head, looking ashamed. "I have placed little value on your friendship with the squaw, merely because she is of another race. Now I see what it means to you . . . and to her. Your Curious Cat does have loyalties, but they lie not with her people, but with you." He reached out to stroke her cheek—something he had not done since he had found Curious Cat in their kitchen.

Lydia touched his hand, knowing all was mended between them.

Of course, the men of Salina were equally skeptical of the threat of Indian attack. But Ben Whitesides had the forceful qualities of a leader, and, once he had assembled them, his newfound conviction in the truth of Curious Cat's story gave strength to his words. When the attack came, the town was prepared, and the Cheyennes were driven off.

In the days that followed, many of the townswomen paid stiff formal calls on Lydia, to thank her for her part in the victory. The awkwardness was dispelled, however, when talk turned to her expected child, and several of the women returned bearing small gifts for the baby. Lydia knew Salina had finally taken her in on the day when Mrs. Ellerbee, wife of the bank president, hesitantly asked if she would consider joining a new musical society the ladies were thinking of forming. And while she realized she would never take as much pleasure in the ladies' refined company as she had in the mornings she'd spent with Curious Cat, she assented readily.

Curious Cat came one last time, on a day when wintry clouds lowered overhead. Lydia was tending to her newborn son in his cradle next to the stove, and she had to raise the window, which had been shut against the chill, to admit her friend.

The squaw went immediately to the cradle. She stared at Ben Junior for a long moment, then said: "Fine papoose. Strong." Quickly she moved on to the stove and inspected the bread that was browning there.

Lydia said: "I'm so glad you've come. I've wanted to thank you. . . ."

Curious Cat cut her short with a gesture of dismissal. She looked around the kitchen, as if to fix it in her mind. Then she said: "Come for good bye."

"But there's no need! You are welcome here anytime."

The Indian woman shook her head sorrowfully. "White Tail go north. I go with. One sleep, then go."

Lydia was overcome with a sharp sense of loss. She moved forward, taking the other woman's hands. "But there is so much I must say to you. . . ."

Curious Cat shook her head again. "One sleep, then go. Come for good bye." Gently she disentwined her fingers from Lydia's. Lydia knew Curious Cat was not one for touching, so she let her go.

The Indian woman glanced at the cradle once more. "Fine papoose. You raise him strong. Brave."

"Yes. I promise I will."

Curious Cat nodded in satisfaction. Then she put her hands to the buffalo horn necklace she still wore and lifted it over her head. She lowered it over Lydia's curls and placed it around her neck, smoothing the collar of her dress over it.

"White sister," she said.

Tears rose to Lydia's eyes. She blinked them away, unable to speak. She had no parting gift, nothing so fine. . . . And then she looked down at her bodice, secured by the soapstone brooch etched with the tree of the prairie, Ben's birthday gift to her. He would approve, think it fitting, too.

With fumbling fingers Lydia undid the brooch and pinned it to the faded calico at Curious Cat's throat. "Not white sister," she said. "True sister."

The Lost Coast

California's Lost Coast is at the same time one of the most desolate and beautiful of shorelines. Northerly winds whip the sand into a dust-devil frenzy; eerie, stationary fogs hang in the trees and distort the driftwood until it resembles the bones of prehistoric mammals; bruised clouds hover above the peaks of the distant King Range, then blow down to sea level and dump icy torrents. But on a fair day the sea and sky show infinite shadings of blue, and the wildflowers are a riot of color. If you wait quietly, you can spot deer, peregrine falcons, foxes, otters, even black bears and mountain lions.

A contradictory and oddly compelling place, this seventy-three-mile stretch of coast southwest of Eureka, where—as with most worthwhile things or people—you must take the bad with the good.

Unfortunately on my first visit there I was taking mostly the bad. Strong wind pushed my MG all over the steep, narrow road, making its hairpin turns even more perilous. Early October rain cut my visibility to a few yards. After I crossed the swollen Bear River, the road continued to twist and wind, and I began to understand why the natives had dubbed it The Wildcat.

Somewhere ahead, my client had told me, was the hamlet of Petrolia—site of the first oil well drilled in California, he'd irrelevantly added. The man was a conservative politician, a former lumber company attorney, and given what I knew of his voting record on the environment, I was certain we disagreed on the desirability of that event, as well as any number of similar issues. But the urgency of the current situation dictated that I keep my opinions to myself, so I'd simply written down the directions he gave me—omitting his travelogue-like asides—and gotten under way.

I drove through Petrolia—a handful of new buildings, since the village had been all but leveled in the disastrous earthquake of 1992—and turned toward the sea on an unpaved road. After two miles I began looking for the orange post that marked the dirt track to the client's cabin.

The whole time I was wishing I was back in San Francisco. This wasn't my kind of case; I didn't like the client, Steve Shoemaker; and even though the fee was good, this was the week I'd scheduled to take off a few personal business days from All Souls Legal Cooperative, where I'm chief investigator. But Jack Stuart, our criminal specialist, had asked me to take on the job as a favor to him. Steve Shoemaker was Jack's old friend from college in Southern California, and he'd asked for a referral to a private detective. Jack owed Steve a favor; I owed Jack several, so there was no way I could gracefully refuse.

But I couldn't shake the feeling that something was wrong with this case. And I couldn't stop wishing that I'd come to the Lost Coast in summertime, with a backpack and in the company of my lover—instead of on a rainy fall afternoon, with a .38 Special, and soon to be in the company of Shoemaker's disagreeable wife, Andrea.

The rain was sheeting down by the time I spotted the orange post. It had turned the hard-packed earth to mud, and my MG's tires sank deep in the ruts, its undercarriage scraping dangerously. I could barely make out the stand of livc oaks and sycamores where the track ended; no way to tell if another vehicle had traveled over it recently.

When I reached the end of the track, I saw onc of those boxy four-wheel-drive wagons—Bronco? Cherokee?—drawn in under the drooping branches of an oak. Andrea Shoemaker's? I'd neglected to get a description from her husband of what she drove. I got out of the MG, turning the hood of my heavy sweater up against the downpour; the wind promptly blew it off. So much for what the catalog had described as "extra protection on those cold nights". I yanked the hood up again and held it there, went around and took my .38 from the trunk and shoved it into the outside flap of my purse. Then I went over and tried the door of the four-wheel drive. Unlocked. I opened it, slipped into the driver's seat.

Nothing identifying its owner was on the seats or in the side pockets, but in the glove compartment I found a registration in the name of Andrea Shoemaker. I rummaged around, came up with nothing else of interest. Then I got out and walked through the trees, looking for the cabin.

Shoemaker had told me to follow a deer track through

the grove. No sign of it in this downpour, no deer, either. Nothing but wind-lashed trees, the oaks pelting me with acorns. I moved slowly through them, swiveling my head from side to side, until I made out a bulky shape tucked beneath the farthest of the sycamores.

As I got closer, I saw the cabin was of plain weathered wood, rudely constructed, with the chimney of a woodstove extending from its composition shingle roof. Small—two or three rooms—and no light showing in its windows. And the door was open, banging against the inside wall. . . .

I quickened my pace, taking the gun from my purse. Alongside the door I stopped to listen. Silence. I had a flashlight in my bag; I took it out. Moved to where I could see inside, then turned the flash on and shone it through the door.

All that was visible was rough board walls, an oil-cloth-covered table and chairs, an ancient woodstove. I stepped inside, swinging the light around. Unlit oil lamp on the table; flower-cushioned wooden furniture of the sort you always find in vacation cabins; rag rugs; shelves holding an assortment of tattered paperbacks, seashells, and driftwood. I shifted the light again, more slowly.

A chair on the far side of the table was tipped over, and a woman's purse lay on the edge of the wood-stove, its contents spilling out. When I got over there, I saw a .32 Iver Johnson revolver lying on the floor.

Andrea Shoemaker owned a .32. She'd told me so the day before.

Two doors opened off the room. Quietly I went to one and tried it. A closet, shelves stocked with staples and canned goods and bottled water. I looked around the room again, listening. No sound but the wail of wind and the pelt of rain on the roof. I stepped to the other door.

A bedroom almost filled wall-to-wall by a king-size bed covered with a goose-down comforter and piled with colorful pillows. Old bureau pushed in one corner, another unlit oil lamp on the single nightstand. Small travel bag on the bed.

The bag hadn't been opened. I examined its contents. Jeans, a couple of sweaters, underthings, toilet articles. Package of condoms. Uhn-huh. She'd come here, as I'd found out, to meet a man. The affairs usually began with a casual pick-up; they were never of long duration; and they all seemed to culminate in a romantic week-end in the isolated cabin.

Dangerous game, particularly in these days when AIDS and the prevalence of disturbed individuals of both sexes threatened. But Andrea Shoemaker had kept her latest date with an even larger threat hanging over her: for the past six weeks, a man with a serious grudge against her husband had been stalking her. For all I knew, he and the date were one and the same.

And where was Andrea now?

This case had started on Wednesday, two days ago, when I'd driven up to Eureka, a lumbering and fishing town on Humboldt Bay. After I passed the Humboldt County line, I began to see huge logging trucks toiling through the mountain passes, shredded curls of red-wood bark trailing in their wakes. Twenty-five miles south of the city itself was the company-owned town of Scotia, mill stacks belching white smoke and filling the air with the scent of freshly cut wood. Yards full of logs waiting to be fed to the mills lined the highway. When I reached Eureka itself, the downtown struck me as curiously quiet; many of the stores were out of business, and the sidewalks were mostly deserted. The recession had hit the lumber industry hard, and the earthquake hadn't helped the area's strapped economy.

I'd arranged to meet Steve Shoemaker at his law offices in Old Town, near the waterfront. It was a picturesque area full of renovated warehouses and interesting shops and restaurants, tricked up for tourists with the inevitable horse-and-carriage rides and T-shirt shops, but still pleasant. Shoemaker's offices were off a cobble-stoned courtyard containing a couple of antique shops and a decorator's showroom.

When I gave my card to the secretary, she said Assemblyman Shoemaker was in conference and asked me to wait. The man, I knew, had lost his seat in the state legislature this past election, so the term of address seemed inappropriate. The appointments of the waiting room struck me as a bit much—brass and mahogany and marble and velvet, plenty of it, the furnishings all antiques that tended to the garish. I sat on a red velvet sofa and looked for something to read. *Architectural Digest, National Review, Foreign*

Affairs—that was it, take it or leave it. I left it. My idea of waiting-room reading is *People*; I love it, but I'm too embarrassed to subscribe.

The minutes ticked by: ten, fifteen, twenty. I contemplated the issue of *Architectural Digest*, then opted instead for staring at a fake Rembrandt on the far wall. Twenty-five, thirty. I was getting irritated now. Shoemaker had asked me to be here by three; I'd arrived on the dot. If this was, as he'd claimed, a matter of such urgency and delicacy that he couldn't go into it on the phone, why was he in conference at the appointed time?

Thirty-five minutes. Thirty-seven. The door to the inner sanctum opened and a woman strode out. A tall woman, with long chestnut hair, wearing a raincoat and black leather boots. Her eyes rested on me in passing—a cool gray, hard with anger. Then she went out, slamming the door behind her.

The secretary—a trim blonde in a tailored suit—started as the door slammed. She glanced at me and tried to cover with a smile, but its edges were strained, and her fingertips pressed hard against the desk. The phone at her elbow buzzed; she snatched up the receiver. Spoke into it, then said to me: "Miz McCone, Assemblyman Shoemaker will see you now." As she ushered me inside, she again gave me her frayed-edge smile.

Tense situation in this office, I thought. Brought on by what? The matter Steve Shoemaker wanted me to investigate? The client who had just made her angry exit? Or something else entirely . . . ?

Shoemaker's office was even more pretentious than the waiting room: more brass, mahogany, velvet, and marble; more fake Old Masters in heavy gilt frames; more antiques; more of everything. Shoemaker's demeanor was not as nervous as his secretary's, but, when he rose to greet me, I noticed a jerkiness in his movements, as if he were holding himself under tight control. I clasped his outstretched hand and smiled, hoping the familiar social rituals would set him more at ease.

Momentarily they did. He thanked me for coming, apologized for making me wait, and inquired after Jack Stuart. After I was seated in one of the client's chairs, he offered me a drink; I asked for mineral water. As he went to a wet bar tucked behind a tapestry screen, I took the opportunity to study him.

Shoemaker was handsome: dark hair, with the gray so artfully interwoven that it must have been professionally dyed. Chiseled features, nice, well-muscled body, shown off to perfection by an expensive blue suit. When he handed me my drink, his smile revealed white, even teeth that I—having spent the greater part of the previous month in the company of my dentist—recognized as capped. Yes, a very good-looking man, politician handsome. Jack's old friend or not, his appearance and manner called up my gut-level distrust.

My client went around his desk and reclaimed his chair. He held a drink of his own—something dark amber—and he took a deep swallow before speaking. The alcohol replenished his vitality some; he drank

116

again, set the glass on a pewter coaster, and said: "Miz McCone, I'm glad you could come up here on such short notice."

"You mentioned on the phone that the case is extremely urgent . . . and delicate."

He ran his hand over his hair—lightly, so as not to disturb its styling. "Extremely urgent and delicate," he repeated, seeming to savor the phrase.

"Why don't you tell me about it?"

His eyes strayed to the half-full glass on the coaster. Then they moved to the door through which I'd entered. Returned to me. "You saw the woman who just left?"

I nodded.

"My wife, Andrea."

I waited.

"She's very angry with me for hiring you."

"She did act angry. Why?"

Now he reached for the glass and belted down its contents. Leaned back and rattled the ice cubes as he spoke. "It's a long story. Painful to me. I'm not sure where to begin. I just . . . don't know what to make of the things that are happening."

"That's what you've hired me to do. Begin anywhere. We'll fill in the gaps later." I pulled a small tape recorder from my bag and set it on the edge of his desk. "Do you mind?"

Shoemaker eyed it warily, but shook his head. After a moment's hesitation, he said: "Someone is stalking my wife."

"Following her? Threatening her?"

"Not following, not that I know of. He writes notes, threatening to kill her. He leaves . . . things at the house. At her place of business. Dead things. Birds, rats, one time a cat. Andrea loves cats. She. . . ." He shook his head, went to the bar for a refill.

"What else? Phone calls?"

"No. One time, a floral arrangement . . . suitable for a funeral."

"Does he sign the notes?"

"John. Just John."

"Does Missus Shoemaker know anyone named John who has a grudge against her?"

"She says no. And I. . . ." He sat down, fresh drink in hand. "I have reason to believe that this John has a grudge against me, is using this harassment of Andrea to get at me personally."

"Why do you think that?"

"The wording of the notes."

"May I see them?"

He looked around, as if he were afraid someone might be listening. "Later. I keep them elsewhere."

Something, then, I thought, that he didn't want his office staff to see. Something shameful, perhaps even criminal.

"OK," I said, "how long has this been going on?"

"About six weeks."

"Have you contacted the police?"

"Informally. A man I know on the force, Sergeant Bob Wolfe. But after he started looking into it, I had to ask him to drop it."

"Why?"

"I'm in a sensitive political position."

"Excuse me if I'm mistaken, Mister Shoemaker, but it's my understanding that you're no longer serving in the state legislature."

"That's correct, but I'm about to announce my candidacy in a special election for a senate seat that's recently been vacated."

"I see. So after you asked your contact on the police force to back off, you decided to use a private investigator, and Jack recommended me. Why not use someone local?"

"As I said, my position is sensitive. I don't want word of this getting out in the community. That's why Andrea is so angry with me. She claims I value my political career more than her life."

I waited, wondering how he'd attempt to explain that away.

He didn't even try, merely went on. "In our . . . conversation just prior to this, she threatened to leave me. This coming week-end she plans to go to a cabin on the Lost Coast that she inherited from her father to . . . as she put it . . . sort things through. Alone. Do you know that part of the coast?"

"I've read some travel pieces on it."

"Then you're aware how remote it is. The cabin's very isolated. I don't want Andrea going there while this John person is on the loose."

"Does she go there often?"

"Fairly often. I don't . . . it's too rustic for me . . . no

119

running water, phone, or electricity. But Andrea likes it. Why do you ask?"

"I'm wondering if John . . . whoever he is . . . knows about the cabin. Has she been there since the harassment began?"

"No. Initially she agreed that it wouldn't be a good idea. But now. . . ." He shrugged.

"I'll need to speak with Missus Shoemaker. Maybe I can reason with her, persuade her not to go until we've identified John. Or maybe she'll allow me to go along as her bodyguard."

"You can speak with her if you like, but she's beyond reasoning with. And there's no way you can stop her or force her to allow you to accompany her. My wife is a strong-willed woman . . . that interior decorating firm across the courtyard is hers, she built it from the ground up. When Andrea decides to do something, she does it. And asks permission from no one."

"Still, I'd like to try reasoning. This trip to the cabin . . . that's the urgency you mentioned on the phone. Two days to find the man behind the harassment before she goes out there and perhaps makes a target of herself."

"Yes."

"Then I'd better get started. That funeral arrangement . . . what florist did it come from?"

Shoemaker shook his head. "It arrived at least five weeks ago, before either of us noticed a pattern to the harassment. Andrea just shrugged it off, threw the wrappings and card away."

"Let's go and look at the notes, then. They're my only lead."

VENGEANCE WILL BE MINE. THE SUDDEN BLOW. THE QUICK ATTACK.
VENGEANCE IS THE PRICE OF SILENCE.

MUTE TESTIMONY PAVES THE WAY TO AN EARLY GRAVE. THE REST IS SILENCE.

A FRESHLY TURNED GRAVE IS SILENT TESTIMONY TO AN OLD WRONG AND ITS AVENGER.

There was more in the same vein—slightly Biblical-flavored and stilted. But chilling to me, even though the safety deposit booth at Shoemaker's bank was overly warm. If that was my reaction, what had these notes done to Andrea Shoemaker? No wonder she was thinking of leaving a husband who cared more for the electorate's opinion than his wife's life and safety.

The notes had been typed without error on an electric machine that had left no such obvious clues as chipped or skewed keys. The paper and envelopes were plain and cheap, purchasable at any discount store. They had been handled, I was sure, by nothing more than gloved hands. No signature—just the typed name, JOHN.

But the writer had wanted the Shoemakers—one of them, anyway—to know who he was. Thus the theme that ran through them all: silence and revenge.

I said: "I take it your contact at the E.P.D. had their lab go over these?"

"Yes. There was nothing. That's why he wanted to probe further . . . something I couldn't permit him to do."

"Because of this revenge-and-silence business. Tell me about it."

Shoemaker looked around furtively. My God, did he think bank employees had nothing better to do with their time than to eavesdrop on our conversation?

"We'll go have a drink," he said. "I know a place that's private."

We went to a restaurant a few blocks away, where Shoemaker had another bourbon and I toyed with a glass of iced tea. After some prodding, he told me his story; it didn't enhance him in my eyes.

Seventeen years ago Shoemaker had been interviewing for a staff attorney's position at a large lumber company. While on a tour of the mills, he witnessed an accident in which a worker named Sam Carding was severely mangled while trying to clear a jam in a bark-stripping machine. Shoemaker, who had worked in the mills summers to pay for his education, knew the accident was due to company negligence, but accepted a handsome job offer in exchange for not testifying for the plaintiff in the ensuing lawsuit. The court ruled against Carding, confined to a wheelchair and in constant pain; a year later, while the case was still under appeal, Carding shot his wife and himself. The couple's three children were given token settlements in exchange for dropping the suit, and then were adopted by relatives in a different part of the country.

"It's not a pretty story, Mister Shoemaker," I said, "and I can see why the wording of the notes might make you suspect there's a connection between it and this harassment. But who do you think John is?"

"Carding's eldest boy. Carding and his family knew I'd witnessed the accident . . . one of his co-workers saw me watching from the catwalk and told him. Later, when I turned up as a senior counsel. . . ." He shrugged.

"But why, after all this time . . . ?"

"Why not? People nurse grudges. John Carding was sixteen at the time of the lawsuit . . . there were some ugly scenes with him, both at my home and my office at the mill. By now he'd be in his forties. Maybe it's his way of acting out some sort of mid-life crisis."

"Well, I'll call my office and have my assistant run a check on all three Carding kids. And I want to speak with Missus Shoemaker . . . preferably in your presence."

He glanced at his watch. "It can't be tonight. She's got a meeting of her professional organization, and I'm dining with my campaign manager."

A potentially psychotic man was threatening Andrea's life, yet they both carried on as usual. Well, who was I to question it? Maybe it was their way of coping.

"Tomorrow, then," I said. "Your home. At the noon hour."

Shoemaker nodded. Then he gave me the address, as well as the names of John Carding's siblings.

I left him on the sidewalk in front of the restaurant—a handsome man whose shoulders now slumped inside his expensive suit coat, shivering in the brisk wind off Humboldt Bay. As we shook hands, I saw that shame made his gaze unsteady, the set of his mouth less than firm.

I knew that kind of shame. Over the course of my career, I'd committed some dreadful acts that years later woke me in the deep of the night to sudden panic. I'd also *not* committed certain acts—failures that woke me to regret and emptiness. My sins of omission were infinitely worse than those of commission, because I knew that if I'd acted, I could have made a difference. Could even have saved a life.

I wasn't able to reach Rae Kelleher, my assistant at All Souls, that evening, and by the time she got back to me the next morning—Thursday—I was definitely annoyed. Still, I tried to keep a lid on my irritation. Rae is young, attractive, and in love. I couldn't expect her to spend her evenings waiting to be of service to her workaholic boss.

I got her started on a computer check on all three Cardings, then took myself to the Eureka P.D. and spoke with Shoemaker's contact, Sergeant Bob Wolfe. Wolfe—a dark-haired, sharp-featured man whose appearance was a good match for his surname—told me he'd had the notes processed by the lab, which had turned up no useful evidence.

"Then I started to probe, you know? When you got a harassment case like this, you look into the victims' private lives."

"And that was when Shoemaker told you to back off?"

"Uhn-huh."

"When was this?"

"About five weeks ago."

"I wonder why he waited so long to hire me. Did he, by any chance, ask you for a referral to a local investigator?"

Wolfe frowned. "Not this time."

"Then you'd referred him to someone before?"

"Yeah, guy who used to be on the force . . . Dave Morrison. Last April."

"Did Shoemaker tell you why he needed an investigator?"

"No, and I didn't ask. These politicians, they're always trying to get something on their rivals. I didn't want any part of it."

"Do you have Morrison's address and phone number handy?"

Wolfe reached into his desk drawer, shuffled things, and flipped a business card across the blotter. "Dave gave me a stack of these when he set up shop," he said. "Always glad to help an old pal."

Morrison was out of town, the message on his answering machine said, but would be back tomorrow afternoon. I left a message of my own, asking him to call me at my motel. Then I headed for the Shoe-makers' home, hoping I could talk some common sense into Andrea.

But Andrea wasn't having any common sense.

She strode around the parlor of their big Victorian—built by one of the city's lumber barons, her husband told me when I complimented them on it—arguing and waving her arms and making scathing statements punctuated by a good amount of profanity. And knocking back martinis, even though it was only a little past noon.

Yes, she was going to the cabin. No, neither her husband nor I was welcome there. No, she wouldn't postpone the trip; she was sick and tired of being cooped up like some kind of zoo animal because her husband had made a mistake years before she'd met him. All right, she realized this John person was dangerous. But she'd taken self-defense classes and owned a .32 revolver. Of course, she knew how to use it. Practiced frequently, too. Women had to be prepared these days, and she was.

But, she added darkly, glaring at her husband, she'd just as soon not have to shoot John. She'd rather send him straight back to Steve and let them settle this score. May the best man win—and she was placing bets on John.

As far as I was concerned, Steve and Andrea Shoe-maker deserved each other.

I tried to explain to her that self-defense classes don't fully prepare you for a paralyzing, heart-pounding encounter with an actual violent stranger. I tried to warn her that the ability to shoot well on a firing range doesn't fully prepare you for pumping a bullet into a human being who is advancing swiftly on you.

I wanted to tell her she was being an idiot.

Before I could, she slammed down her glass and stormed out of the house.

Her husband replenished his own drink and said: "Now do you see what I'm up against?"

I didn't respond to that. Instead, I said: "I spoke with Sergeant Wolfe earlier."

"And?"

"He told me he referred you to a local private investigator, Dave Morrison, last April."

"So?"

"Why didn't you hire Morrison for this job?"

"As I told you yesterday, my. . . ."

"Sensitive position, yes."

Shoemaker scowled.

Before he could comment, I asked: "What was the job last April?"

"Nothing to do with this matter."

"Something to do with politics?"

"In a way."

"Mister Shoemaker, hasn't it occurred to you that a political enemy may be using the Carding case as a smoke screen? That a rival's trying to throw you off balance before this special election?"

"It did, and . . . well, it isn't my opponent's style. My

God, we're civilized people. But those notes . . . they're the work of a lunatic."

I wasn't so sure he was right—both about the notes being the work of a lunatic and politicians being civilized people—but I merely said: "OK, you keep working on Missus Shoemaker. At least persuade her to let me go to the Lost Coast with her. I'll be in touch." Then I headed for the public library.

After a few hours of ruining my eyes at the microfilm machine, I knew little more than before. Newspaper accounts of the Carding accident, lawsuit, and murder-suicide didn't differ substantially from what my client had told me. Their coverage of the Shoemakers' activities was only marginally interesting.

Normally I don't do a great deal of background investigation on clients, but, as Sergeant Wolfe had said, in a case like this, where one or both of them was a target, a thorough look at careers and lifestyles was mandatory. The papers described Steve as a straight-forward, effective assemblyman who took a hard, conservative stance on such issues as welfare and the environment. He was strongly pro-business, particularly the lumber industry. He and his "charming and talented wife" didn't share many interests: Steve hunted and golfed; Andrea was a "generous supporter of the arts" and a "lavish party-giver". An odd couple, I thought, and odd people to be friends of Jack Stuart, a liberal who'd chosen to dedicate his career to representing the underdog.

Back at the motel, I put in a call to Jack. Why, I asked him, had he remained close to a man who was so clearly his opposite?

Jack laughed. "You're trying to say politely that you think he's a pompous, conservative ass."

"Well. . . ."

"OK, I admit it . . . he is. But back in college, he was a mentor to me. I doubt I would have gone into the law if it hadn't been for Steve. And we shared some good times, too . . . one summer we took a motorcycle trip around the country, like something out of EASY RIDER without the tragedy. I guess we stay in touch because of a shared past."

I was trying to imagine Steve Shoemaker on a motorcycle; the picture wouldn't materialize. "Was he always so conservative?" I asked.

"No, not until he moved back to Eureka and went to work for that lumber company. Then . . . I don't know. Everything changed. It was as if something happened that took all the fight out of him."

What had happened, I thought, was trading another man's life for a prestigious job.

Jack and I chatted for a moment longer, and then I asked him to transfer me to Rae. She hadn't turned up anything on the Cardings yet, but was working on it. In the meantime, she added, she'd taken care of what correspondence had come in, dealt with seven phone calls, entered next week's must-dos in the call-up file she'd created for me, and found a remedy for the blight that was affecting my rubber plant.

With a pang, I realized that the office ran just as well—better, perhaps—when I wasn't there. It would keep functioning smoothly without me for weeks, months, maybe years.

Hell, it would probably keep functioning smoothly even if I were dead.

In the morning I opened the Yellow Pages to "florists" and began calling each that was listed. While Shoemaker had been vague on the date his wife received the funeral arrangement, surely a customer who wanted one sent to a private home, rather than a mortuary, would stand out in the order-taker's mind. The listing was long, covering a relatively wide area; it wasn't until I reached the Rs and my watch showed nearly eleven o'clock that I got lucky.

"I don't remember any order like that in the past six weeks," the clerk at Rainbow Florists said, "but we had one yesterday, was delivered this morning."

I gripped the receiver harder. "Will you pull the order, please?"

"I'm not sure I should. . . ."

"Please. You could help save a woman's life."

Quick intake of breath, then his voice filled with excitement; he'd become part of a real-life drama. "One minute. I'll check." When he came back on the line, he said: "Thirty-dollar standard condolence arrangement, delivered this morning to Mister Steven Shoemaker. . . ."

"*Mister?* Not Missus or Miz?"

"Mister, definitely. I took the order myself." He read off the Shoemakers' address.

"Who placed it?"

"A kid. Came in with cash and written instructions."

Standard ploy—hire a kid off the street so nobody can identify you. "Thanks very much."

"Aren't you going to tell me . . . ?"

I hung up and dialed Shoemaker's office. His secretary told me he was working at home today. I dialed the home number. Busy. I hung up, and the phone rang immediately. Rae, with information on the Cardings.

She'd traced Sam Carding's daughter and younger son. The daughter lived near Cleveland, Ohio, and Rae had spoken with her on the phone. John, his sister had told her, was a drifter and an addict; she hadn't seen him in more than ten years. When Rae reached the younger brother at his office in L.A., he told her the same, adding that he assumed John had died years ago.

I thanked Rae and told her to keep on it. Then I called Shoemaker's number again. Still busy, time to go over there.

Shoemaker's Lincoln was parked in the drive of the Victorian, a dusty Honda motorcycle beside it. As I rang the doorbell, I again tried to picture a younger, free-spirited Steve bumming around the country on a bike with Jack, but the image simply wouldn't come clear. It took Shoemaker a while to answer the door, and, when he saw me, his mouth pulled down in displeasure.

"Come in, and be quick about it," he told me. "I'm on an important conference call."

I was quick about it. He rushed down the hallway to what must be a study, and I went into the parlor where we'd talked the day before. Unlike his offices, it was exquisitely decorated, calling up images of the days of the lumber barons. Andrea's work, probably. Had she also done his offices? Perhaps their gaudy décor was her way of getting back at a husband who put his political life ahead of their marriage?

It was at least a half an hour before Shoemaker finished with his call. He appeared in the archway leading to the hall, somewhat disheveled, running his fingers through his hair. "Come with me," he said. "I have something to show you."

He led me to a large kitchen at the back of the house. A floral arrangement sat on a granite-topped center island: white lilies with a single red rose. Shoemaker handed me the card. My sympathy on your wife's passing. It was signed: John.

"Where's Missus Shoemaker?" I asked.

"Apparently she went out to the coast last night. I haven't seen her since she walked out on us at the noon hour."

"And you've been home the whole time?"

He nodded. "Mainly on the phone."

"Why didn't you call me when she didn't come home?"

"I didn't realize she hadn't until mid-morning. We have separate bedrooms, and Andrea comes and goes as she pleases. Then this arrangement arrived, and my conference call came through. . . ." He shrugged, spreading his hands helplessly.

"All right," I said. "I'm going out there whether she likes it or not. And I think you'd better clear up whatever you're doing here and follow. Maybe your showing up there will convince her you care about her safety, make her listen to reason."

As I spoke, Shoemaker had taken a fifth of Tanqueray gin and a jar of Del Prado Spanish olives from a Lucky sack that sat on the counter. He opened a cupboard, reached for a glass.

"No," I said. "This is no time to have a drink."

He hesitated, then replaced the glass, and began giving me directions to the cabin. His voice was flat, and his curious travelogue-like digressions made me feel as if I were listening to a tape of a *National Geographic* special. Reality, I thought, had finally sunk in, and it had turned him into an automaton.

I had one stop to make before heading out to the coast, but it was right on my way. Morrison Investigations had its office in what looked to be a former motel on Highway 101, near the outskirts of the city. It was a neighborhood of fast-food restaurants and bars, thrift shops and marginal businesses. Besides the detective agency, the motel's cinder-block units housed an insurance brokerage, a secretarial service, two accountants, and a palm reader. Dave Morrison, who was just arriving as I pulled into the parking area, was a bit of a surprise: in his mid-forties, wearing one small gold earring, and a short ponytail. I wondered what Steve Shoemaker had made of him.

Morrison showed me into a two-room suite crowded with computer equipment and file cabinets and furniture that looked as if he might have hauled it down the street from the nearby Thrift Emporium. When he noticed me studying him, he grinned easily. "I know I don't look like a former cop. I worked undercover Narcotics my last few years on the force. Afterwards, I realized I was comfortable with the uniform." His gestures took in his lumberjack's shirt, work-worn jeans, and boots.

I smiled in return, and he cleared some files off a chair so I could sit.

"So you're working for Steve Shoemaker," he said.

"I understand you did, too."

He nodded. "Last April and again around the beginning of August."

"Did he approach you about another job after that?"

He shook his head.

"And the jobs you did for him were . . . ?"

"You know better than to ask that."

"I was going to ask, were they completed to his satisfaction?"

"Yes."

"Do you have any idea why Shoemaker would go to the trouble of bringing me up from San Francisco when he had an investigator here whose work satisfied him?"

Head shake.

"Shoemaker told me the first job you did for him had to do with politics."

The corner of his mouth twitched "In a matter of speaking." He paused, shrewd eyes assessing me. "How come you're investigating your own client?"

"It's that kind of case. And something feels wrong. Did you get that sense about either of the jobs you took on for him?"

"No." Then he hesitated, frowning. "Well, maybe. Why don't you just come out and ask what you want to? If I can, I'll answer."

"OK . . . did either of the jobs have to do with a man named John Carding?"

That surprised him. After a moment he asked a question of his own. "He's still trying to trace Carding?"

"Yes.

Morrison got up and moved toward the window, stopped and drummed his fingers on top of a file cabinet. "Well, I can save you further trouble. John Carding is untraceable. I tried every way I know . . . and that's every way there is. My guess is that he's dead, years dead."

"And when was it you tried to trace him?"

"Most of August."

Weeks before Andrea Shoemaker had begun to receive the notes from "John". Unless the harassment had started earlier? No, I'd seen all the notes, examined their postmarks. Unless he'd thrown away the first ones, as she had the card that came with the funeral arrangement?

"Shoemaker tell you why he wanted to find Carding?" I asked.

"Uhn-uh."

"And your investigation last April had nothing to do with Carding?"

At first I thought Morrison hadn't heard the question. He was looking out the window, then he turned, expression thoughtful, and opened one of the drawers of the filing cabinet beside him. "Let me refresh my memory," he said, taking out a couple of folders. I watched as he flipped through them, frowning.

Finally he said: "I'm not gonna ask about your case. If something feels wrong, it could be because of what I turned up last spring . . . and that I don't want on my conscience." He closed one file, slipped it back in the cabinet, then glanced at his watch. "Damn! I just remembered I've got to make a call." He crossed to the desk, set the open file on it. "I better do it from the other room. You stay here, find something to read."

I waited until he'd left, then went over and picked up the file. Read it with growing interest and began putting things together. Andrea had been discreet about her extramarital activities, but not so discreet that a competent investigator like Morrison couldn't uncover them.

When Morrison returned, I was ready to leave for the Lost Coast.

"Hope you weren't bored," he said.

"No. I'm easily amused. And, Mister Morrison, I owe you a dinner."

"You know where to find me. I'll look forward to seeing you again."

And now that I'd reached the cabin, Andrea had disappeared. The victim of violence, all signs indicated. But the victim of whom? John Carding—a man no one had seen or heard from for over ten years? Another man named John, one of her cast-off lovers? Or . . . ?

What mattered now was to find her.

I retraced my steps, turning up the hood of my sweater again as I went outside. Circled the cabin, peering through the lashing rain. I could make out a couple of other small structures back there: outhouse and shed. The outhouse was empty. I crossed to the shed. Its door was propped open with a log, as if she'd been getting fuel for the stove.

Inside, next to a neatly stacked cord of wood, I found her.

She lay face down on the hard-packed dirt floor, blue-jeaned legs splayed, plaid-jacketed arms flung above her head, chestnut hair cascading over her back. The little room was silent, the total silence that surrounds the dead. Even my own breath was stilled; when it came again, it sounded obscenely loud.

I knelt beside her, forced myself to perform all the checks I've made more times than I could have imagined. No breath, no pulse, no warmth to the skin. And the rigidity. . . .

On the average—although there's a wide variance— *rigor mortis* sets in to the upper body five to six hours after death; the whole body is usually affected within eighteen hours. I backed up and felt the lower part of her body. Rigid—*rigor* was complete. I straightened, went to stand in the doorway. She'd probably been dead since midnight. And the cause? I couldn't see any wounds, couldn't further examine her without disturbing the scene. What I should be doing was getting in touch with the sheriff's department.

Back to the cabin. Emotions tore at me: anger, regret, and—yes—guilt that I hadn't prevented this. But I also sensed that I *couldn't* have prevented it. I, or someone like me, had been an integral component from the first.

In the front room I found some kitchen matches, and lit the oil lamp. Then I went around the table and looked down at where her revolver lay on the floor. More evidence—don't touch it. The purse and its spilled contents rested near the edge of the stove. I inventoried the items visually: the usual make-up, brush, comb, spray perfume, wallet, keys, roll of postage stamps, daily planner that flopped open to show pockets for business cards and receipts. And a loose piece of paper. . . .

Lucky Food Center, it said at the top. Perhaps she'd stopped to pick up supplies before leaving Eureka, the date and time on this receipt might indicate how long she'd remained in town before storming out on her husband and me.

I picked it up. At the bottom I found yesterday's date and the time of purchase: 9:14 p.m.

KY SERV DELI . . . CRABS . . . WINE . . . DEL PRADO OLIVE . . . LG RED DEL . . . ROUGE ET NOIR . . . BAKERY . . . TANQ GIN. . . .

A sound outside. Footsteps slogging through the mud. I stuffed the receipt into my pocket.

Steve Shoemaker came through the open door in a hurry, rain hat pulled low on his forehead, droplets sluicing down his chiseled nose. He stopped when he saw me, looked around. "Where's Andrea?"

I said: "I don't know."

"What do you mean, you don't know? Her Bronco's outside. That's her purse on the stove."

"And her bag's on the bed, but she's nowhere to be found."

Shoemaker arranged his face into lines of concern. "There's been a struggle here."

"Appears that way."

"Come on, we'll look for her. She may be in the outhouse or the shed. She may be hurt. . . ."

"It won't be necessary to look." I had my gun out of my purse now, and I leveled it at him. "I know you killed your wife, Shoemaker."

"What?"

"Her body's where you left it last night. What time did you kill her? How?"

His faked concern shaded into panic. "I didn't. . . ."

"You did."

No reply. His eyes moved from side to side—calculating, looking for a way out.

I added: "You drove her here in the Bronco, with

your motorcycle inside. Arranged things to simulate a struggle, put her in the shed, then drove back to town on the bike. You shouldn't have left the bike outside the house where I could see it. It wasn't muddy out here last night, but it sure was dusty."

"Where are these baseless accusations coming from? John Carding. . . ."

"Is untraceable, probably dead, as you know from the check Dave Morrison ran."

"He told you. . . . What about the notes, the flowers, the dead things . . . ?"

"Sent by you."

"Why would I do that?"

"To set the scene for getting rid of a chronically unfaithful wife who had potential to become a political embarrassment."

He wasn't cracking, though. "Granted, Andrea had her problems. But why would I rake up the Carding matter?"

"Because it would sound convincing for you to admit what you did all those years ago. God knows it convinced me. And I doubt the police would ever have made the details public. Why destroy a grieving widower and prominent citizen? Particularly when they'd never find Carding or bring him to trial. You've got one problem, though . . . me. You never should have brought me in to back up your scenario."

He licked his lips, glaring at me. Then he drew himself up, leaned forward aggressively—a posture the attorneys at All Souls jokingly refer to as their "litigator's mode".

140

"You have no proof of this," he said firmly, jabbing his index finger at me. "No proof whatsoever."

"Deli items, crabs, wine, apples," I recited. "Del Prado Spanish olives, Tanqueray gin."

"What the hell are you talking about?"

"I have Andrea's receipt for the items she bought at Lucky yesterday, before she stopped home to pick up her week-end bag. None of these things is here in the cabin."

"So?"

"I know that at least two of them . . . the olives and the gin . . . are at your house in Eureka. I'm willing to bet they all are."

"What if they are? She did some shopping for me yesterday morning. . . ."

"The receipt is dated yesterday *evening,* nine-fourteen p.m. I'll quote you, Shoemaker. 'Apparently she went out to the coast last night. I haven't seen her since she walked out on us at the noon hour.' But you claim you didn't leave home after noon."

That did it; that opened the cracks. He stood for a moment, then half collapsed into one of the chairs and put his head in his hands.

The next summer, after I testified at the trial in which Steve Shoemaker was convicted of the first-degree murder of his wife, I returned to the Lost Coast—with a backpack, without the .38, and in the company of my lover. We walked sand beaches under skies that showed infinite shadings of blue; we made love in

141

fields of wildflowers; we waited quietly for the deer, falcons, and foxes.

I'd already taken the bad from this place; now I could take the good.

Forbidden Things

All the years that I was growing up in a poor suburb of Los Angeles, my mother would tell me stories of the days I couldn't remember when we lived with my father on the wild north coast. She'd tell of a gray, misty land suddenly made brilliant by quicksilver flashes off the sea; of white sand beaches that would disappear in a storm, then emerge strewn with driftwood and treasures from foreign shores; of a deeply forested ridge of hills where, so the Pomo Indians claimed, spirits walked by night.

Our cabin nestled on that ridge, high above the little town of Camel Rock and the humpbacked offshore mass that inspired its name. The cabin, built to last by my handyman father, was of local redwood, its foundation sunk deep in bedrock. There was a woodstove and home-woven curtains. There were stained-glass windows and a sleeping loft; there was. . . .

Although I had no recollection of this place we'd left when I was two, it somehow seemed more real to me than our shabby pink bungalow with the cracked sidewalk out front and the packed-dirt yard out back. I'd lie in bed at night feeling the heat from the woodstove, watching the light as it filtered through the stained-glass panels, listening to the wind buffet our secure aerie. I was sure I could smell my mother's baking bread, hear the deep rumble of my father's voice. But no matter how hard I tried, I could not call up the image of my father's face, even though a stiff and formal portrait of him sat on our coffee table.

When I asked my mother why she and I had left a place of quicksilver days and night-walking spirits, she'd grow quiet. When I asked where my father was now, she'd turn away. As I grew older I realized there were shadows over our departure—shadows in which forbidden things stood, still and silent.

Is it any wonder that when my mother died—young, at forty-nine, but life hadn't been kind to her and heart trouble ran in the family—is it any wonder that I packed everything I cared about and went back to the place of my birth to confront those forbidden things?

I'd located Camel Rock on the map when I was nine, tracing the coast highway with my finger until it reached a jutting point of land north of Fort Bragg. Once this had been logging country—hardy men working the cross-cut saw and jackscrew in the forests, bull teams dragging their heavy loads to the coast, fresh-cut logs thundering down the chutes to schooners that lay at anchor in the coves below. But by the time I was born, lumbering was an endangered industry. Today, I knew, the voice of the chain saw was stilled and few logging trucks rumbled along the highway. Legislation to protect the environment, coupled with a severe construction slump, had all but killed the old economy. Instead new enterprises had sprung up: wineries, mushroom, garlic, and herb farms, tourist shops, and bed-and-breakfasts. These were only marginally profitable, however; the north coast was financially strapped.

I decided to go anyway.

It was a good time for me to leave southern California. Two failed attempts at college, a ruined love affair, a series of slipping-down jobs—all argued for radical change. I'd had no family except my mother; even my cat had died the previous October. As I gave notice at the coffee shop where I'd been waitressing, disposed of the contents of the bungalow, and turned the keys back to the landlord, I said no good byes. Yet I left with hope of a welcome. Maybe there would be a place for me in Camel Rock. Maybe someone would even remember my family and fill in the gaps in my early life.

I know now that I was really hoping for a reunion with my father.

Mist blanketed the coast the afternoon I drove my old Pinto over the bridge spanning the mouth of the Deer River and into Camel Rock. Beyond sandstone cliffs the sea lay, flat and seemingly motionless. The town—a strip of buildings on either side of the highway with dirt lanes straggling up toward the hills—looked deserted. A few drifting columns of wood smoke, some lighted signs in shop windows, a hunched and bundled figure walking along the shoulder—these were the only signs of life. I drove slowly, taking it all in: a supermarket, some bars, a little mall full of tourist shops. Post office, laundromat, defunct real estate agency, old sagging hotel that looked to be the only real lodging place. When I'd gone four blocks and passed the last gas station and the cable TV company, I ran out of town. I U-turned, went back to the hotel, and parked my car between two pickups out front.

For a moment I sat behind the wheel, feeling flat. The town didn't look like the magical place my mother had described; if anything, it was seedier than the suburb I'd left yesterday. I had to force myself to get out, and, when I did, I stood beside the Pinto, staring up at the hotel. Pale green with once white trim, all of it blasted and faded by the elements. An inscription above its front door gave the date it was built—1879, the height of last century's logging boom. Neon beer signs flashed in its lower windows; gulls perched along the peak of its roof, their droppings splashed over the steps and front porch. I watched as one soared in for a landing, crying shrilly. Sea breeze ruffled my short blond hair, and I smelled fish and brine.

The smell of the sea had always delighted me. Now it triggered a sense of connection to this place. I thought: *Home*.

The thought lent me the impetus to take out my overnight bag and carried me over the threshold of the hotel. Inside was a dim lobby that smelled of dust and cat. I peered through the gloom but saw no one. Loud voices came from a room to the left, underscored by the clink of glasses and the thump and clatter of dice rolling; I went over, looked in, and saw an old-fashioned tavern, peopled mainly by men in work clothes. The ship's clock that hung crooked behind the bar said 4:20. Happy hour got under way early in Camel Rock.

There was a public phone on the other side of the lobby. I crossed to it and opened the thin county directory, aware that my fingers were trembling. No listing for my father. No listing for anyone with my last name. More disappointed than I had any right to be, I replaced the book and turned away.

Just then a woman came out of a door under the steep staircase. She was perhaps in her early sixties, tall and gaunt, with tightly permed, gray curls and a face lined by weariness. When she saw me, her pale eyes registered surprise. "May I help you?"

I hesitated, the impulse to flee the shabby hotel and drive away from Camel Rock nearly irresistible. Then I thought: *Come on, give the place a chance.* "Do you have a room available?"

"We've got nothing but available rooms." She smiled wryly and got a card for me to fill out. Lacking any other, I put down my old address and formed the letters of my signature—Ashley Heikkinen—carefully. I'd always hated my last name; it seemed graceless and misshapen beside my first. Now I was glad it was unusual; maybe someone here in town would recognize it. The woman glanced disinterestedly at the card, however, then turned away and studied a rack of keys.

"Front room or back room?"

"Which is more quiet?"

"Well, in front you've got the highway noise, but

there's not much traffic at night. In the back you've got the boys"—she motioned at the door to the tavern—"scrapping in the parking lot at closing time."

Just what I wanted—a room above a bar frequented by quarrelsome drunks. "I guess I'll take the front."

The woman must have read my expression. "Oh, honey, don't you worry about them. They're not so bad, but there's nobody as contentious as an out-of-work logger who's had one over his limit."

I smiled and offered my Visa card. She shook her head and pointed to a cash only sign. I dug in my wallet and came up with the amount she named. It wasn't much, but I didn't have much to begin with. There had been a small life insurance policy on my mother, but most of it had gone toward burying her. If I was to stay in Camel Rock, I'd need a job.

"Are a lot of people around here out of work?" I asked as the woman wrote up a receipt.

"Loggers, mostly. The type who won't bite the bullet and learn another trade. But the rest of us aren't in much better shape."

"Have you heard of any openings for a waitress or a bartender?"

"For yourself?"

"Yes. If I can find a job, I may settle here."

Her hand paused over the receipt book. "Honey, why on earth would you want to do that?"

"I was born here. Maybe you knew my parents . . . Melinda and John Heikkinen?"

She shook her head and tore the receipt from the

book. "My husband and me, we just moved down here last year from Del Norte County . . . things're even worse up there, believe me. We bought this hotel because it was cheap and we thought we could make a go of it."

"Have you?"

"Not really. We don't have the wherewithal to fix it up, so we can't compete with the new motels or bed-and-breakfasts. And we made the mistake of giving bar credit to the locals."

"That's too bad," I said. "There must be some jobs available, though. I'm a good waitress, a fair bartender. And I . . . like people," I added lamely.

She smiled, the lines around her eyes crinkling kindly. I guessed she'd presented meager credentials a time or two herself. "Well, I suppose you could try over at the mall. Barbie Cannon's been doing real good with her Beachcomber Shop, and the tourist season'll be here before we know it. Maybe she can use some help."

I thanked her and took the room key she offered, but, as I picked up my bag, I thought of something else. "Is there a newspaper in town?"

"As far as I know, there never has been. There's one of those little county shoppers, but it doesn't have ads for jobs, if that's what you're after."

"Actually I'm trying to locate . . . a family member. I thought if there was a newspaper, I could look through their back issues. What about long-time residents of the town? Is there anybody who's an amateur historian, for instance?"

149

"Matter of fact, there is. Gus Galick. Lives on his fishing trawler, the *Irma*, down at the harbor. Comes in here regular."

"How long has he lived here?"

"All his life."

Just the person I wanted to talk with.

The woman added: "Gus is away this week, took a charter party down the coast. I think he said he'd be back next Thursday."

Another disappointment. I swallowed it, told myself the delay would give me time to settle in and get to know the place of my birth. And I'd start by visiting the Beachcomber Shop.

The shop offered exactly the kind of merchandise its name implied: seashells, driftwood, inexpert carvings of gulls, grebes, and sea lions. Postcards and calendars and T-shirts and paperback guidebooks. Shell jewelry, paperweights, ceramic whales and dolphins. Nautical toys and candles and wind chimes. All of which were totally predictable, but the woman who popped up from behind the counter was anything but.

She was very tall, well over six feet, and her black hair stood up in long, stiff spikes. A gold ring pierced her left nostril, and several others hung from either earlobe. She wore a black leather tunic with metal studs, over lacy black tights and calf-high boots. In L.A., I wouldn't have given her a second glance, but this was Camel Rock. Such people weren't supposed to happen here.

The woman watched my reaction, then threw back her head and laughed throatily. I felt a blush begin to creep over my face.

"Hey don't worry about it," she told me. "You should see how I scare the little bastards who drag their parents in here, whining about how they absolutely *have* to have a blow-up Willie the Whale."

"Uh, isn't that bad for business?"

"Hell, no. Embarrasses the parents and they buy twice as much as they would've."

"Oh."

"So . . . what can I do for you?"

"I'm looking for Barbie Cannon."

"You found her." She flopped onto a stool next to the counter, stretching out her long legs.

"My name's Ashley Heikkinen." I watched her face for some sign of recognition. There wasn't any, but that didn't surprise me; Barbie Cannon was only a few years older than I—perhaps thirty—and too young to remember a family that had left so long ago. Besides, she didn't look as if she'd been born and raised here.

"I'm looking for a job," I went on, "and the woman at the hotel said you might need some help in the shop."

She glanced around at the merchandise that was heaped haphazardly on the shelves and spilled over onto the floor here and there. "Well, Penny's right . . . I probably do." Then she looked back at me. "You're not local."

"I just came up from L.A."

"Me, too, about a year ago. There're a fair number of us transplants, and the division between us and the locals is pretty clear-cut."

"How so?"

"A lot of the natives are down on their luck, resentful of the newcomers, especially ones like me, who're doing well. Oh, some of them're all right . . . they understand that the only way for the area to survive is to restructure the economy. But most of them are just sitting around the bars mumbling about how the spotted owl ruined their lives and hoping the timber industry'll make a comeback . . . and that ain't gonna happen. So why're *you* here?"

"I was born in Camel Rock. And I'm sick of southern California."

"So you decided to get back to your roots."

"In a way."

"You alone?"

I nodded.

"Got a place to stay?"

"The hotel, for now."

"Well, it's not so bad, and Penny'll extend credit if you run short. As for a job. . . ." She paused, looking around again. "You know. I came up here thinking I'd work on my photography. The next Ansel Adams and all that." She grinned self-mockingly. "Trouble is, I got to be such a successful businesswoman that I don't even have time to load my camera. Tell you what . . . . why don't we go over to the hotel tavern, tilt a few, talk it over?"

"Why not?" I said.

Mist hugged the tops of the sequoias and curled in tendrils around their trunks. The mossy ground under my feet was damp and slick. I hugged my hooded sweatshirt against the chill and moved cautiously up the incline from where I'd left the car on an overgrown logging road. My soles began to slip, and I crouched, catching at a stump for balance. The wet fronds of a fern brushed my cheek.

I'd been tramping through the hills for over two hours, searching every lane and dirt track for the burned-out cabin that Barbie Cannon had photographed shortly after her arrival in Camel Rock last year. Barbie had invited me to her place for dinner the night before, after we'd agreed on the terms of my new part-time job, and in the course of the evening she'd shown me her portfolio of photographs. One, a grimy black-and-white image of a ruin, so strongly affected me that I'd barely been able to sleep. This morning I'd dropped by the shop and gotten Barbie to draw me a map of where she'd found it, but her recollection was so vague that I might as well have had no map at all.

I pushed back to my feet and continued climbing. The top of the rise was covered by a dense stand of sumac and bay laurel; the spicy scent of the laurel leaves mixed with stronger odors of redwood and eucalyptus. The mixed bouquet triggered the same sense of connection that I'd felt as I stood in front of the hotel the previous afternoon. I breathed deeply, then elbowed through the dense branches.

From the other side of the thicket I looked down on a sloping meadow splashed with the brilliant yellow-orange of California poppies. More sequoias crowned the ridge on its far side, and through their branches I caught a glimpse of the flat, leaden sea. A stronger feeling of familiarity stole over me. I remembered my mother saying: "In the spring, the meadow was full of poppies, and you could see the ocean from our front steps. . . ."

The mist was beginning to break up overhead. I watched a hawk circle against a patch of blue high above the meadow, then wheel and flap away toward the inland hills. He passed over my head, and I could feel the beating of his great wings. I turned, my gaze following his flight path. . . .

And then I spotted the cabin, overgrown and wrapped in shadow, only yards away. Built into the downward slope of the hill, its moss-covered foundations were anchored in bedrock, as I'd been told. But the rest was only blackened and broken timbers, a collapsed shake roof on which vegetation had taken root, a rusted stove chimney about to topple, empty windows and doors.

I drew in my breath and held it for a long moment. Then I slowly moved forward.

Stone steps, four of them. I counted as I climbed. Yes, you could still see the Pacific from here, the meadow, too. And the opening was where the door had been. Beyond it, nothing but a concrete slab covered the débris. Plenty of evidence that picnickers had been here.

I stepped over the threshold.

One big empty room. Nothing left, not even the mammoth iron woodstove. Vines growing through the timbers, running across the floor. And at the far side, a collapsed heap of burned lumber—the sleeping loft?

Something crunched under my foot. I looked down, squatted, poked at it gingerly with my fingertip. Glass, green glass. It could have come from a picnicker's wine bottle. Or it could have come from a broken stained-glass window.

I stood, coldness upon my scalp and shoulder blades. Coldness that had nothing to do with the sea wind that bore the mist from the coast. I closed my eyes against the shadows and the ruin. Once again I could smell my mother's baking bread, hear my father's voice. Once again I thought: *Home.*

But when I opened my eyes, the warmth and light vanished. Now all I saw was the scene of a terrible tragedy.

"Barbie," I said, "what do you know about the North-coast Lumber Company?"

She looked up from the box of wind chimes she was unpacking. "Used to be the big employer around here."

"Where do they have their offices? I couldn't find a listing in the county phone book."

"I hear they went bust in the 'Eighties."

"Then why would they still own land up in the hills?"

"Don't know. Why?"

I hesitated. Yesterday, the day after I'd found the cabin, I'd driven down to the county offices at Fort Bragg and spent the entire afternoon poring over the land plats for this area. The place where the ruin stood appeared to belong to the lumber company. There was no reason I shouldn't confide in Barbie about my search, but something held me back. After a moment I said: "Oh, I saw some acreage that I might be interested in buying."

She raised her eyebrows; the extravagant white eye shadow and bright-red lipstick that she wore today made her look like an astonished clown. "On what I'm paying you for part-time work, you're buying land?"

"I've got some savings from my mom's life insurance." That much was true, but the small amount wouldn't buy even a square foot of land.

"Huh." She went back to her unpacking. "Well, I don't know for a fact that Northcoast did go bust. Penny told me that the owner's widow is still alive. Used to live on a big estate near here, but a long time ago she moved down the coast to that fancy retirement community at Timber Point. Maybe she could tell you about this acreage."

"What's her name, do you know?"

"No, but you could ask Penny. She and Crane bought the hotel from her."

• • •

"Madeline Carmichael," Penny said. "Lady in her late fifties. She and her husband used to own a lot of property around here."

"You know her, then."

"Nope, never met her. Our dealings were through a realtor and her lawyer."

"She lives down at Timber Point?"

"Uhn-huh. The realtor told us she's a recluse, never leaves her house, and has everything she needs delivered."

"Why, do you suppose?"

"Why not? She can afford it. Oh, the realtor hinted that there's some tragedy in her past, but I don't put much stock in that. I'll tell you"—her tired eyes swept the dingy hotel lobby—"if I had a beautiful home and all that money, I'd never go out, either."

Madeline Carmichael's phone number and address were unlisted. When I drove down to Timber Point the next day, I found high grape-stake fences and a gatehouse; the guard told me that Mrs. Carmichael would see no one who wasn't on her visitor list. When I asked him to call her, he refused. "If she was expecting you," he said, "she'd have sent your name down."

Penny had given me the name of the realtor who handled the sale of the hotel. He put me in touch with Mrs. Carmichael's lawyer in Fort Bragg. The attorney told me he'd check about the ownership of the land and get back to me. When he did, his reply was terse:

The land was part of the original Carmichael estate; title was held by the nearly defunct lumber company; it was not for sale.

So why had my parents built their cabin on the Carmichael estate? Were my strong feelings of connection to the burned-out ruin in the hills false?

Maybe, I told myself, it was time to stop chasing memories and start building a life for myself here in Camel Rock. Maybe it was best to leave the past alone.

The following week-end brought the kind of quicksilver days my mother had told me about, and in turn they lured tourists in record numbers. We couldn't restock the Beachcomber Shop's shelves fast enough. On the next Wednesday—Barbie's photography day—I was unpacking fresh merchandise and filling in where necessary while waiting for the woman Barbie bought her driftwood sculptures from to make a delivery. Business was slack in the late-afternoon hours. I moved slowly, my mind on what to wear to a dinner party being given that evening by some new acquaintances who ran an herb farm. When the bell over the door jangled, I started.

It was Mrs. Fleming, the driftwood lady. I recognized her by the big plastic wash basket of sculptures that she toted. A tiny white-haired woman, she seemed too frail for such a load. I moved to take it from her.

She resisted, surprisingly strong. Her eyes narrowed, and she asked: "Where's Barbie?"

"Wednesday's her day off."

"And who are you?"

"Ashley Heikkinen. I'm Barbie's part-time. . . ."

"*What* did you say?"

"My name is Ashley Heikkinen. I just started here last week."

Mrs. Fleming set the basket on the counter and regarded me sternly, spots of red appearing on her cheeks. "Just what are you up to, young woman?"

"I don't understand."

"Why are you using that name?"

"Using . . . ? It's my name."

"It most certainly is not! This is a very cruel joke."

The woman had to be unbalanced. Patiently I said: "Look, my name really is Ashley Heikkinen. I was born in Camel Rock but moved away when I was two. I grew up outside Los Angeles, and, when my mother died, I decided to come back here."

Mrs. Fleming shook her head, her lips compressed, eyes glittering with anger.

"I can prove who I am," I added, reaching under the counter for my purse. "Here's my identification."

"Of course, you have identification. Everyone knows how to obtain that under the circumstances."

"What circumstances?"

She turned and moved toward the door. "I can't imagine what you possibly hope to gain by this charade, young woman, but you can be sure I'll speak to Barbie about you."

"Please, wait!"

She pushed through the door, and the bell above it

jangled harshly as it slammed shut. I hurried to the window and watched her cross the parking lot in a vigorous stride that belied her frail appearance. As she turned at the highway, I looked down and saw I had my wallet out, prepared to prove my identity.

Why, I wondered, *did I feel compelled to justify my existence to this obviously deranged stranger?*

The dinner party that evening was pleasant, and I returned to the hotel at a little after midnight with the fledgling sense of belonging that making friends in a strange place brings. The fog was in thick, drawn by hot inland temperatures. It put a gritty sheen on my face, and, when I touched my tongue to my lips, I tasted the sea. I locked the Pinto and started across the rutted parking lot to the rear entrance. Heavy footsteps came up behind me.

Conditioned by many years in L.A., I already held my car key in my right hand, tip out as a weapon. I glanced back and saw a stocky, bearded man bearing down on me. When I side-stepped and turned, he stopped, and his gaze moved to the key. He'd been drinking—beer, and plenty of it.

From the tavern, I thought. *Probably came out to the parking lot because the rest room's in use and he couldn't wait.* "After you," I said, opening the door for him.

He stepped inside the narrow, dim hallway. I let him get a ways ahead, then followed. The door stuck, and I turned to give it a tug. The man reversed, came up swiftly, and grasped my shoulder.

"Hey!" I said.

He spun me around and slammed me against the wall. "Lady, what the hell're you after?"

"Let go of me!" I pushed at him.

He pushed back, grabbed my other shoulder, and pinned me there. I stopped struggling, took a deep breath, told myself to remain calm.

"Not going to hurt you, lady," he said. "I just want to know what your game is."

Two lunatics in one day. "What do you mean . . . game?"

"My name is Ashley Heikkinen," he said in a falsetto, then dropped to his normal pitch. "Who're you trying to fool? And what's in it for you?"

"I don't. . . ."

"Don't give me that! You might be able to stonewall an old lady like my mother. . . ."

"Your mother?"

"Yeah, Janet Fleming. You expect her to believe you, for Christ's sake? What you did, you upset her plenty. She had to take one of the Valiums the doctor gave me for my bad back."

"I don't understand what your mother's problem is."

"Jesus, you're a cold bitch! Her own goddaughter, for Christ's sake, and you expect her to *believe* you?"

"Goddaughter?"

His face was close to mine now; hot beer breath touched my cheeks. "My ma's goddaughter was Ashley Heikkinen."

161

"That's impossible! I never had a godmother. I never met your mother until this afternoon."

The man shook his head. "I'll tell you what's impossible . . . Ashley Heikkinen appearing in Camel Rock after all these years. Ashley's dead. She died in a fire when she wasn't even two years old. My ma ought to know . . . she identified the body."

A chill washed over me from my scalp to my toes. The man stared, apparently recognizing my shock as genuine. After a moment I asked: "Where was the fire?"

He ignored the question, frowning. "Either you're a damned good actress or something weird's going on. Can't have two people born with that name. Not in Camel Rock."

"Where was the fire?"

He shook his head again, this time as if to clear it. His mouth twisted, and I feared he was going to be sick. Then he let go of me and stumbled through the door to the parking lot. I released my breath in a long sigh and slumped against the wall. A car started outside. When its tires had spun on the gravel and its engine revved on the highway, I pushed myself upright and went along the hall to the empty lobby. A single bulb burned in the fixture above the reception desk, as it did every night. The usual sounds of laughter and conversation came from the tavern.

Everything seemed normal. Nothing was. I ran upstairs to the shelter of my room.

After I'd double-locked the door, I turned on the

overhead and crossed to the bureau and leaned across it toward the streaky mirror. My face was drawn and unusually pale.

Ashley Heikkinen dead?

Dead in a fire when she wasn't quite two years old?

I closed my eyes, picturing the blackened ruin in the hills above town. Then I opened them and stared at my frightened face. It was the face of a stranger.

"If Ashley Heikkinen is dead," I said, "then who am *I*?"

Mrs. Fleming wouldn't talk to me. When I got to her cottage on one of the packed-dirt side streets after nine the next morning, she refused to open the door and threatened to run me off with her dead husband's shotgun. "And don't think I'm not a good marks-woman," she added.

She must have gone straight to the phone, because Barbie was hanging up when I walked into the Beachcomber Shop a few minutes later. She frowned at me and said: "I just had the most insane call from Janet Fleming."

"About me?"

"How'd you guess? She was giving me all this stuff about you not being who you say you are and the 'real Ashley Heikkinen' dying in a fire when she was a baby. Must be going around the bend."

I sat down on the stool next to the counter. "Actually there might be something to what she says." And then I told her all of it: my mother's stories, the forbidden things that went unsaid, the burned-out cabin in the hills, my encounters with Janet Fleming and her son. "I tried to talk with Missus Fleming this morning," I finished, "but she threatened me with a shotgun."

"And she's been known to use that gun, too. You must've really upset her."

"Yes. From something she said yesterday afternoon, I gather she thinks I got hold of the other Ashley's birth certificate and created a set of fake ID around it."

"You sound like you believe there *was* another Ashley."

"I saw that burned-out cabin. Besides, why would Missus Fleming make something like that up?"

"But you recognized the cabin, both from my photograph and when you went there. You said it felt like home."

"I recognized it from my mother's stories, that's true. Barbie, I've lived those stories for most of my life. You know how kids sometimes get the notion that they're so special they can't really belong to their parents, that they're a prince or princess who was given to a servant couple to raise?"

"Oh, sure, we all went through that stage. Only in my case, I was Mick Jagger's love child, and someday he was going to acknowledge me and give me all his money."

"Well, my mother's stories convinced me that I didn't really belong in a downscale tract in a crappy valley town. They made me special, somebody who came from a magical place. And I dreamed of it every night."

"So you're saying that you only recognized the cabin from the images your mother planted in your mind?"

"It's possible."

Barbie considered. "OK, I'll buy that. And here's a scenario that might fit . . . after the fire, your parents moved away. That would explain why your mom didn't want to talk about why they left Camel Rock. And they had another child . . . you. They gave you Ashley's name and her history. It wasn't right, but grief does crazy things to otherwise sane people."

It worked—but only in part. "That still doesn't explain what happened to my father and why my mother would never talk about him."

"Maybe she was the one who went crazy with grief, and after a while he couldn't take it any .more, so he left."

She made it sound so logical and uncomplicated. But I'd known the quality of my mother's silences; there was more to them than Barbie's scenario encompassed.

I bit my lip in frustration. "You know, Missus Fleming could shed a lot of light on this, but she refuses to deal with me."

"Then find somebody who will."

"Who?" I asked. And then I thought of Gus Galick, the man Penny had told me about who had lived in Camel Rock all his life. "Barbie, do you know Gus Galick?"

"Sure. He's one of the few old-timers around here

that I've really connected with. Gus builds ships in bottles. I sold some on consignment for him last year. He used to be a rum-runner during Prohibition, has some great stories about bringing in cases of Canadian booze to the coves along the coast."

"He must be older than God."

"Older than God and sharp as a tack. I bet he could tell you what you need to know."

"Penny said he was away on some charter trip."

"Was, but he's back now. I saw the *Irma* in her slip at the harbor when I drove by this morning."

Camel Rock's harbor was a sheltered cove with a bait shack and a few slips for fishing boats. Of them, Gus Galick's *Irma* was by far the most shipshape, and her captain was equally trim, with a shock of silvery-gray hair and leathery tan skin. I didn't give him my name, just identified myself as a friend of Penny and Barbie. Galick seemed to take people at face value, though; he welcomed me on board, took me below-decks, and poured me a cup of coffee in the cozy wood-paneled cabin. When we were seated on either side of the teak table, I asked my first question.

"Sure, I remember the fire on the old Carmichael estate," he said. "Summer of 'Seventy-One. Both the father and the little girl died."

I gripped the coffee mug tighter. "The father died, too?"

"Yeah. Heikkinen, his name was Norwegian, maybe. I don't recall his first name, or the little girl's."

166

"John and Ashley."

"These people kin to you?"

"In a way. Mister Galick, what happened to Melinda, the mother?"

He thought. "Left town, I guess. I never did see her after the double funeral."

"Where are John and Ashley buried?"

"Graveyard of the Catholic church." He motioned toward the hills, where I'd seen its spire protruding through the trees. "Carmichaels paid for everything, of course. Guilt, I guess."

"Why guilt?"

"The fire started on their land. Was the father's fault . . . John Heikkinen's, I mean . . . but, still, they'd sacked him, and that was why he was drinking so heavy. Fell asleep with the doors to the woodstove open, and before he could wake up, the place was a furnace."

The free-flowing information was beginning to overwhelm me. "Let me get this straight . . . John Heikkinen worked for the Carmichaels?"

"Was their caretaker. His wife looked after their house."

"Where was she when the fire started?"

"At the main house, washing up after the supper dishes. I heard she saw the flames, run down there, and tried to save her family. The Carmichaels held her back till the volunteer fire department could get there . . . they knew there wasn't any hope from the beginning."

167

I set the mug down, gripped the table's edge with icy fingers.

Galick leaned forward, eyes concerned. "Something wrong, miss? Have I upset you?"

"I shook my head. "It's just . . . a shock, hearing about it after all these years." After a pause, I asked: "Did the Heikkinens have any other children?"

"Only the little girl who died."

I took out a photograph of my mother and passed it over to him. It wasn't a good picture, just a snap of her on the steps of our stucco bungalow down south. "Is this Melinda Heikkinen?"

He took a pair of glasses from a case on the table, put them on, and looked closely at it. Then he shrugged and handed it back to me. "There's some resemblance, but. . . . She looks like she's had a hard life."

"She did." I replaced the photo in my wallet. "Can you think of anyone who could tell me more about the Heikkinens?"

"Well, there's Janet Fleming. She was Missus Heikkinen's aunt and the little girl's godmother. The mother was so broken up that Janet had to identify the bodies, so I guess she'd know everything there is to know about the fire."

"Anyone else?"

"Well, of course there's Madeline Carmichael. But she's living down at Timber Point now, and she never sees anybody."

"Why not?"

168

"I've got my own ideas on that. It started after her husband died. Young man, only in his fifties. Heart attack." Galick grimaced. "Carmichael was one of these pillars of the community, never drank, smoked, or womanized. Keeled over at a church service in 'Seventy-Five. Me, I've lived a gaudy life, as they say. Even now I eat and drink all the wrong things, and I like a cigar after dinner. And I just go on and on. Tells you a lot about the randomness of it all."

I didn't want to think about that randomness; it was much too soon after losing my own mother to an untimely death for that. I asked: "About Missus Carmichael . . . it was her husband's death that turned her into a recluse?"

"No, miss." He shook his head firmly. "My idea is that his dying was just the last straw. The seeds were planted when their little girl disappeared three years before that."

"Disappeared?"

"It was in 'Seventy-Two, the year after the fire. The little girl was two years old, a change-of-life baby. Abigail, she was called. Abby, for short. Madeline Carmichael left her in her playpen on the verandah of their house, and she just plain vanished. At first they thought it was a kidnapping . . . the lumber company was failing, but the family still had plenty of money. But nobody ever made a ransom demand, and they never did find a trace of Abby or the person who took her."

The base of my spine began to tingle. As a child,

I'd always been smaller than others of my age. Slower in school, too. The way a child might be if she was a year younger than the age shown on her birth certificate.

Abigail Carmichael, I thought. *Abby, for short.*

The Catholic churchyard sat tucked back against a eucalyptus grove; the trees' leaves caught the sunlight in a subtle shimmer, and their aromatic buds were thick under my feet. An iron fence surrounded the graves, and unpaved paths meandered among the mostly crumbling headstones. I meandered, too, shock gradually leaching away to depression. The foundations of my life were as tilted as the oldest grave marker, and I wasn't sure I had the strength to construct a new one.

But I'd come here with a purpose, so finally I got a grip on myself and began covering the cemetery in a grid pattern.

I found them in the last row, where the fence backed up against the eucalyptus. Two small headstones set side-by-side. John and Ashley. There was room to John's right for another grave, one that now would never be occupied.

I knelt and brushed a curl of bark from Ashley's stone. The carving was simple, only her name and the dates. She'd been born April 6, 1969, and died February 1, 1971.

I knelt there for a long time. Then I said good bye and went home.

The old Carmichael house sat at the end of a chained-off drive that I'd earlier taken for a logging road. It was a wonder I hadn't stumbled across it in my search for the cabin. Built of dark timber and stone, with a wide verandah running the length of the lower story, it once might have been imposing. But now the windows were boarded, birds roosted in its eaves, and all around it the forest encroached. I followed a cracked flagstone path through a lawn long gone to weeds and wildflowers to the broad front steps. Stood at their foot, my hand on the cold wrought-iron railing.

Could a child of two retain memories? I'd believed so before, but mine had turned out to be false, spoon-fed to me by the woman who had taken me from this verandah twenty-four years earlier. All the same, something in this lonely place spoke to me; I felt a sense of peace and safety that I'd never before experienced.

I hadn't known real security; my mother's and my life together had been too uncertain, too difficult, too shadowed by the past. Those circumstances probably accounted for my long string of failures, my inability to make my way in the world. A life built on lies and forbidden things was bound to go nowhere.

And yet it hadn't had to be that way. All this could have been mine, had it not been for a woman unhinged by grief. I could have grown up in this once lovely home, surrounded by my real parents' love. Perhaps if I had, my father would not have died of an untimely heart attack, and my birth mother would not have become a recluse. A sickening wave of anger swept over me, followed by a deep sadness. Tears came to my eyes, and I wiped them away.

I couldn't afford to waste time crying. Too much time had been wasted already.

To prove my real identity, I needed the help of Madeline Carmichael's attorney, and he took a good deal of convincing. I had to provide documentation and witnesses to my years as Ashley Heikkinen before he would consent to check Abigail Carmichael's birth records. Most of the summer went by before he broached the subject to Mrs. Carmichael. But blood composition and the delicate whorls on feet and fingers don't lie; finally, on a bright September afternoon, I arrived at Timber Point—alone, at the invitation of my birth mother.

I was nervous and gripped the Pinto's wheel with damp hands as I followed the guard's directions across a rolling seaside meadow to the Carmichael house. Like the others in this exclusive development, it was of modern design, with a silvery wood exterior that blended with the sawgrass and Scotch broom. A glass wall faced the Pacific, reflecting sun glints on the water. Along the shoreline a flock of pelicans flew south in loose formation.

I'd worn my best dress—pink cotton, too light for the season, but it was all I had—and had spent a ridiculous amount of time on my hair and make-up.

As I parked the shabby Pinto in the drive, I wished I could make it disappear. My approach to the door was awkward; I stumbled on the unlandscaped ground and almost turned my ankle. The uniformed maid who admitted me gave me the kind of glance that once, as a hostess at a coffee shop, I'd reserved for customers without shirt or shoes. She showed me to a living room facing the sea and went away.

I stood in the room's center on an Oriental carpet, unsure whether to sit or stand. Three framed photographs on a grand piano caught my attention; I went over and looked at them. A man and a woman, middle-aged and handsome. A child, perhaps a year old, in a striped romper. The child had my eyes.

"Yes, that's Abigail." The throaty voice—smoker's voice—came from behind me. I turned to face the woman in the photograph. Older now, but still handsome, with upswept creamy white hair and pale porcelain skin, she wore a long caftan in some sort of soft champagne-colored fabric. No reason for Madeline Carmichael to get dressed; she never left the house.

She came over to me and peered at my face. For a moment her eyes were soft and questioning, then they hardened and looked away. "Please," she said, "sit down over here."

I followed her to two matching brocade settees positioned at right angles to the seaward window. We sat, one on each, with a coffee table between us. Mrs. Carmichael took a cigarette from a silver box on the table and lit it with a matching lighter.

Exhaling and fanning the smoke away, she said: "I have a number of things to say to you that will explain my position in this matter. First, I believe the evidence you've presented. You are my daughter Abigail. Melinda Heikkinen was very bitter toward my husband and me . . . if we hadn't dismissed her husband, he wouldn't have been passed out from drinking when the fire started. If we hadn't kept her late at her duties that night, she would have been home and able to prevent it. If we hadn't stopped her from plunging into the conflagration, she might have saved her child. That, I suppose, served to justify her taking our child as a replacement."

She paused to smoke. I waited.

"The logic of what happened seems apparent at this remove," Mrs. Carmichael added, "but at the time we didn't think to mention Melinda as a potential suspect. She'd left Camel Rock the year before . . . even her aunt, Janet Fleming, had heard nothing from her. My husband and I had more or less put her out of our minds. And, of course, neither of us was thinking logically at the time."

I was beginning to feel uneasy. She was speaking so analytically and dispassionately—not at all like a mother who had been reunited with her long lost child.

She went on: "I must tell you about our family. California pioneers on both sides. The Carmichaels were lumber barons. My family were merchant princes engaging in the China trade. Abigail was the last of both lines, born to carry on our tradition. Surely you can understand why this matter is so . . . difficult."

She was speaking of Abigail as someone separate from me. "What matter?" I asked.

"That rôle in life, the one Abigail was born to, takes a certain type of individual. My Abby, the child I would have raised had it not been for Melinda Heikkinen, would not have turned out so. . . ." She bit her lower lip, looked away at the sea.

"So what, Missus Carmichael?"

She shook her head, crushing out her cigarette.

A wave of humilation swept over me. I glanced down at my cheap pink dress, at a chip in the polish on my thumbnail. When I raised my eyes, my birth mother was examining me with faint distaste.

I'd always had a temper; now it rose, and I gave in to it. "So what, Missus Carmichael?" I repeated. "So *common?*"

She winced but didn't reply.

I said: "I suppose you think it's your right to judge a person on her appearance or her financial situation. But you should remember that my life hasn't been easy . . . not like yours. Melinda Heikkinen could never make ends meet. We lived in a valley town east of L.A. She was sick a lot. I had to work from the time I was fourteen. There was trouble with gangs in our neighborhood."

Then I paused, hearing myself. No, I would not do this. I would not whine or beg.

"I wasn't brought up to complain," I continued, "and

I'm not complaining now. In spite of working, I grad-
uated high school with honors. I got a small scholar-
ship, and Melinda persuaded me to go to college. She
helped out financially when she could. I didn't finish,
but that was my own fault. Whatever mistakes I've
made are my own doing, not Melinda's. Maybe she
told me lies about our life here on the coast, but they
gave me something to hang on to. A lot of the time
they were all I had, and now they've been taken from
me. But I'm still not complaining."

Madeline Carmichael's dispassionate façade
cracked. She closed her eyes, compressed her lips.
After a moment she said: "How can you defend that
woman?"

"For twenty-four years she was the only mother I
knew."

Her eyes remained closed. She said: "Please, I will
pay you any amount of money if you will go away and
pretend this meeting never took place."

For a moment I couldn't speak. Then I exclaimed: "I
don't want your money! This is not about money!"

"What, then?"

"What do I want? I thought I wanted my real
mother."

"And now that you've met me, you're not sure you
do." She opened her eyes, looked directly into mine.
"Our feelings aren't really all that different, are they,
Abigail?"

I shook my head in confusion.

Madeline Carmichael took a deep breath. "Abigail,

you say you lived on Melinda's lies, that they were something to sustain you?"

I nodded.

"I've lived on lies, too, and they sustained *me*. For twenty-three years I've put myself to sleep with dreams of our meeting. I woke to them. No matter what I was doing, they were only a fingertip's reach away. And now they've been taken from me, as yours have. My Abby, the daughter I pictured in those dreams, will never walk into this room and make everything all right. Just as the things you've dreamed of are never going to happen."

I looked around the room—at the grand piano, the Oriental carpets, the antiques, and exquisite art objects. Noticed for the first time how stylized and sterile it was, how the cold expanse of glass beside me made the sea blinding and bleak.

"You're right," I said, standing up. "Even if you were to take me in and offer me all this, it wouldn't be the life I wanted."

Mrs. Carmichael extended a staying hand toward me.

I stepped back. "No. And don't worry . . . I won't bother you again."

As I went out into the quicksilver afternoon and shut the door behind me, I thought that even though Melinda Heikkinen had given me a different life, she'd also offered me dreams to soften the hard times and love to ease my passage. My birth mother hadn't even offered me coffee or tea.

On a cold, rainy December evening, Barbie Cannon and I sat at a table near the fireplace in the hotel's tavern, drinking red wine in celebration of my good fortune.

"I can't believe," she said for what must have been the dozenth time, "that old lady Carmichael up and gave you her house in the hills."

"Any more than you can believe I accepted it."

"Well, I thought you were too proud to take her money."

"Too proud to be bought off, but she offered the house with no strings attached. Besides, it's in such bad shape that I'll probably be fixing it up for the rest of my life."

"And she probably took a big tax write-off on it. No wonder rich people stay rich." Barbie snorted. "By the way, how come you're still calling yourself Ashley Heikkinen?"

I shrugged. "Why not? It's been my name for as long as I can remember. It's a good name."

"You're acting awfully laid back about this whole thing."

"You didn't see me when I got back from Timber Point. But I've worked it all through. In a way, I understand how Missus Carmichael feels. The house is nice, but anything else she could have given me isn't what I was looking for."

"So what *were* you looking for?"

I stared into the fire. Madeline Carmichael's porcelain face flashed against the background of the flames. Instead of anger I felt a tug of pity for her: a lonely woman waiting her life out, but really as dead and gone as the merchant princes, the lumber barons, the old days on this wild north coast. Then I banished the image and pictured, instead, the faces of the friends I'd made since coming to Camel Rock: Barbie, Penny and Crane, the couple who ran the herb farm, Gus Galick, and . . . now . . . Janet Fleming and her son, Stu. Remembered all the good times: dinners and walks on the beach, Penny and Crane's fortieth wedding anniversary party, Barbie's first photographic exhibit, a fishing trip on Gus's trawler. And thought of all the good times to come.

"What was I looking for?" I said. "Something I found the day I got here."

Knives at Midnight

My eyes were burning, and I felt not unlike a creature that spends a great deal of its life underground. I marked the beat-up copy of last year's STANDARD CALIFORNIA CODES that I'd scrounged up at a used bookstore on Adams Avenue, then shut it. When I stood up, my limbs felt as if I were emerging from the creature's burrow. I stretched, smiling.

Well, McCone, I told myself, *at last one of your peculiarities is going to pay-off.*

For years, I'd taken what many considered a strange pleasure in browsing through the tissue-thin pages of both the civil and penal codes. I had learned many obscure facts. For instance: It is illegal to trap birds in a public cemetery; anyone advertising merchandise that is made in whole or in part by prisoners must insert the words "convict-made" in the ad copy; stealing a dog worth $400 is grand theft. Now I could add another esoteric statute to my store of knowledge, only this one promised a big pay-off.

Somebody who thought himself above the law was about to go down—and I was the one who would topple him.

Two nights earlier, I'd flown into San Diego's Lindbergh Field from my home base in San Francisco. Flown in on a perilous approach that always makes me, holder of both a single- and a multi-engine rating, wish I didn't know quite so much about pilot error. On top of a perfectly natural edginess, I was aggravated with myself for giving in to my older brother John's plea. The case he wanted me to take on for some friends sounded like one where every lead comes to a dead-end; besides, I was afraid that in my former hometown I'd become embroiled in some family crisis. The McCone clan attracts catastrophe the way normal people attract stray kittens.

John was waiting for me at the curb in his old red International Scout. When he saw me, he jumped out and enveloped me in a bear hug that made me drop both my purse and my briefcase. My travel bag swung around and whacked him on his back; he released me, grunting.

"You're looking good," he said, stepping back.

"So're you." John's a big guy—six foot, four—and sometimes he bulks up from the beer he's so fond of. But now he was slimmed down to muscle and sported a new closely cropped beard. Only his blond hair resisted taming.

He grabbed my bag, tossed it into the Scout, and motioned for me to climb aboard. I held my ground. "Before we go any place . . . you didn't tell Pa I was coming down, did you?"

"No."

"Ma and Melvin? Charlene and Ricky?"

"None of them."

"Good. Did you make me a motel reservation and reserve a rental car?"

"No."

181

"I asked you. . . ."

"You're staying at my place."

"John! Don't you remember . . . ?"

"Yeah, yeah. Don't involve the people you care about in something that could get dangerous. I heard all about that."

"And it *did* get dangerous."

"Not very. Anyway, you're staying with me. Get in."

John can be as stubborn as I when he makes up his mind. I opted for the path of least resistance. "OK, I'll stay tonight . . . only. But what am I supposed to drive while I'm here?"

"I'll loan you the Scout."

I frowned. It hadn't aged well since I last borrowed it.

He added: "I could go along and help you out."

"John!"

He started the engine and edged into the flow of traffic. "You know, I missed you." Reaching over and ruffling my hair, he grinned broadly. "McCone and McCone . . . the detecting duo. Together again."

I heaved a martyred sigh and buckled my seat belt.

The happy tone of our reunion dissipated when we walked into the living room of John's little stucco house in nearby Lemon Grove. His old friends, Bryce and Mari Winslip, sat on the sofa in front of the corner fireplace; their hollow eyes reflected weariness and pain and—when they saw me—a kind of hope that I immediately feared was misplaced. While John made the introductions and fetched wine for me and freshened the Winslips' drinks, I studied them.

Both were a fair number of years older than my brother, perhaps in their early sixties. John had told me on the phone that Bryce Winslip was the painting contractor who had employed him during his apprenticeship; several years ago, he'd retired and they'd moved north to Oregon. Bryce and Mari were white-haired and had the bronzed, tough-skinned look of people who spent a lot of time outdoors. I could tell that customarily they were clear-eyed, mentally acute, and vigorous. But not tonight.

Tonight the Winslips were gaunt-faced and red-eyed; they moved in faltering sequences that betrayed their age. Tonight they were drinking straight whiskey, and every word seemed an effort. Small wonder: they were hurting badly because their only child, Troy, was violently dead.

Yesterday morning, twenty-five-year-old Troy Winslip's body had been found by the Tijuana, Mexico authorities in a parking lot near the bullring at the edge of the border town. He had been stabbed seventeen times. Cause of death: exsanguination. Estimated time of death: midnight. There were no witnesses, no suspects, no known reason for the victim to have been in that place. Although Troy was a San Diego resident and a student at San Diego State, the SDPD could do no more than urge the Tijuana authorities to pursue an investigation and report their findings. The TPD, which would have been overworked even if it wasn't notoriously corrupt, wasn't about to devote time to the murder of a *gringo* who shouldn't have been down there in the middle of the night anyway. For all practical purposes, case closed.

So John had called me, and I'd opened my own case file.

When we were seated, I said to the Winslips: "Tell me about Troy. What sort of person was he?"

They exchanged glances. Mari cleared her throat. "He was a good boy . . . man. He'd settled down and was attending college."

"Studying what?"

"Communications. Radio and TV."

"You say he'd 'settled down'. What does that mean?"

Again they exchanged glances. Bryce said: "After high school, he had some problems that needed to be worked through . . . one of the reasons we moved north. But he's been fine for at least five years now."

"Could you be more specific about these problems?"

"Well, Troy was using drugs."

"Marijuana? Cocaine?"

"Both. When we moved to Oregon, we put him into a good treatment facility. He made excellent progress. After he was released, he went to school at Eugene, but three years ago he decided to come back to San Diego."

"A mistake," Mari said.

"He was a grown man . . . we couldn't stop him,"

184

her husband responded defensively. "Besides, he was doing well, making good grades. There was no way we could have predicted that . . . this would happen."

Mari shrugged.

I asked: "Where was Troy living?"

"He shared a house on Point Loma with another student."

"I'll need the address and the roommate's name. What else can you tell me about Troy?"

Bryce said: "Well, he is . . . was athletic. He liked to sail and play tennis." He looked at his wife.

"He was very articulate," she added. "He had a beautiful voice and would have done well in radio or television."

"Do you know any of his friends here?"

"No, I'm not even sure of the roommate's name."

"What about women? Was he going with anyone? Engaged?"

Head shakes.

"Anything else?"

Silence.

"Well," Bryce said after a moment, "he was a very private person. He didn't share many of the details of his life with us, and we respected that."

I was willing to bet that the parents hadn't shared many details of their life with Troy, either. The Winslips struck me as one of those couples who have formed a closed circle that admits no one, not even their own offspring. The shared glances, their body language, the way they consulted non-verbally before

185

answering my questions—all that pointed to a self-sufficient system. I doubted they'd known their son very well at all, and probably hadn't even realized they were shutting him out.

Bryce Winslip leaned forward, obviously awaiting some response on my part to what he and Mari had told me.

I said: "I have to be frank with you. Finding out what happened to Troy doesn't look promising. But I'll give it a try. John explained about my fee?"

They nodded.

"You'll need to sign one of my standard contracts, as well as a release giving me permission to enter Troy's home and go through his personal effects." I took the forms from my briefcase and began filling them in.

After they'd put their signatures on the forms and Bryce had written me a check as a retainer, the Winslips left for their hotel. John fetched me another glass of wine and a beer for himself and sat in the place Mari had vacated, propping his feet on the raised hearth.

"So," he said, "how're we going to go about this?"

"You mean how am I going to go about this. First, I will check with the SDPD for details on the case. Do you remember Gary Viner?"

"That dumb-looking friend of Joey's from high school?"

All of our brother Joey's friends had been dumb-looking. "Sandy-haired guy, one of the auto shop crowd."

"Oh, yeah. He used to work on Joey's car in front of the house and ogle you when he thought you weren't looking."

I grinned. "That's the one. He used to ogle me during cheerleading, too. When I was down here on that kidnapping case a couple of years ago, he told me I had the prettiest bikini pants of anybody on the squad."

John scowled impatiently, like a proper big brother. "So what's this underwear freak got to do with the Winslip case?"

"Gary's on Homicide with the SDPD now. It's always best to check in with the local authorities when you're working a case on their turf, so I'll stop by his office in the morning, see what he's got from the TJ police."

"Well, just don't wear a short skirt. What should I do while you're seeing him?"

"Nothing. Afterward, *I* will visit Troy's house, talk with the roommate, try to get a list of his friends, and find out more about him. Plus go to State and see what I can dig up there."

"What about me?"

"You will tend to Mister Paint." Mr. Paint was the contracting business he operated out of his home shop and office.

John's lower lip pushed out sulkily.

I said: "How about dinner? I'm starving."

He brightened some. "Mexican?"

"Sure."

"I'll drive."

"OK."

"You'll pay."

"John!"

"Consider it a finder's fee."

Gary Viner hadn't changed since I'd seen him a couple of years earlier, but he was very different from the high school kid I remembered. Gaining weight and filling out had made him more attractive; he'd stopped hiding his keen intelligence and learned to tone down his ogling to subtly speculative looks that actually flattered me. Unfortunately he had no more information on the Winslip murder than what John had already told me.

"Is it OK if I look into this for the parents?" I asked him.

"Feel free. It's not our case, anyway. You go down there"—he motioned in the general direction of Baja, California—"you might want to check in with the TJ authorities."

"I won't be going down unless I come up with something damned good up here."

"Well, good luck, and keep me posted." As I started out of his cubicle, Gary added: "Hey, McCone . . . the last time I saw you, you never did answer my question."

"Which is?"

"Can you still turn a cartwheel?"

I grinned at him. "You bet I can. And my bikini pants are still the prettiest ever."

It made me feel good to see a tough homicide cop blush.

• • •

My first surprise of the day was Troy Winslip's house. It was enormous, sprawling over a double lot that commanded an impressive view of San Diego Bay and Coronado Island. Stucco and brick and half timbers, with a terraced back yard landscaped in brilliantly flowering ice-plant, it must have been at least six thousand square feet, give or take a few.

A rich roommate? Many rich roommates? Whatever, it sure didn't resemble the ramshacklc brown-shingled house that I'd shared with what had seemed a cast of thousands when I was at UC Berkeley.

I rang the bell several times and got no response, so I decided to canvass the neighbors. No one was home at the houses on either side, but across the street I got lucky. The stoop-shouldered man who came to the door was around seventy and proved to like the sound of his own voice.

"Winslip? Sure, I know him. Nice young fellow. He's owned the place for about a year now."

"You're sure he owns it?"

"Yes. I knew the former owners. Gene and Alice Farr . . . nice people, too, but that big house was too much for them, so they sold and bought one of those condos. They told me Winslip paid cash."

Cash? Such a place would go for many hundreds of thousands. "What about his roommate? Do you also know him?"

The old man leered at me. "Roommate? Is that what you call them these days? Well, he's a she. The ladies come and go over there, but none're very permanent. This last one, I'd say she's been there eight, nine weeks."

"Do you know her name?"

He shook his head. "She's a good-looking one, though . . . long red hair, kind of willowy."

"And do you know what either she or Mister Winslip do for a living?"

"Not her, no. And if he does anything, he's never talked about it. I suspect he inherited his money. He's home a lot, when he's not sailing his boat."

"Where does he keep his boat?"

"Glorietta Bay Marina, over on Coronado." The man frowned now, wrinkles around his eyes deepening. "What's this all about, anyway?"

"Troy Winslip's been murdered, and I'm investigating it."

"What?"

"You didn't read about it in the paper?"

"I don't bother with the paper. Don't watch TV, either. With my arthritis, I'm miserable enough . . . I don't need other humans' misery heaped on top of that."

"You're a wise man," I told him, and hurried back where I'd left the Scout.

Glorietta Bay Marina sits at the top of the Silver Strand, catty-corner from the Victorian towers of the Hotel Del Coronado. It took me more than half an hour to get there from Point Loma, and, when I drove into the parking lot, I spotted John leaning against his motorcycle. He waved and started toward me.

I pulled into a space and jumped out of the Scout. "What the hell are *you* doing here?"

"Nice way to greet somebody who's helping you out. While you were futzing around at the police department and Troy's place, I went over to State. Talked with his advisor. She says he dropped out after one semester."

"So how did that lead you here?"

"The advisor sails, and she sees him here off and on. He owns a boat, the *Windsong*."

"And I suppose you've already checked it out."

"No, but I did talk with the marina manager. He says he'll let us go aboard if you show him your credentials and the release from Bryce and Mari."

"Good work," I said grudgingly. "You know," I added as we started walking toward the manager's office, "it's odd that Troy would berth the boat here."

"Why?"

"He lived on Point Loma, not far from the Shelter Island yacht basin. Why would he want to drive all the way around the bay and across the Coronado Bridge when he could have berthed her within walking distance of his house?"

"No slips are available over there? No, that can't be . . . I've heard the marina's going hungry in this economy."

"Interesting, huh? And wait till you hear what else. . . ." I stopped in my tracks and glared at him. "Dammit, you've done it again!"

"Done what? I didn't do anything! What did I do?"

"You know *exactly* what you've done."

John's smile was smug.

I sighed. "All right, other half of the 'detecting duo' . . . lead me to the manager."

My unwanted assistant and I walked along the outer pier toward the *Windsong*'s slip. The only sounds were the cries of seabirds and the rush of traffic on the strand. Our footsteps echoed on the aluminum walkways and set them to bucking on a slight swell. No one was around this Wednesday morning except for a pair of artists, sketching near the office; the boats were buttoned up tightly, their sails furled in sea-blue covers. Troy Winslip's yawl was a big one, some thirty feet. I crossed the plank and stepped aboard; John followed.

"Wonder where he got his money," he said. "Bryce and Mari're well-off, but not wealthy."

"I imagine he had his ways." I tried the companionway door and found it locked.

"What now?" my brother asked. "Standing around on deck isn't going to tell us anything."

"No." I felt in my bag and came up with my set of lock picks.

John's eyes widened. "Aren't those illegal?"

"Not strictly." I selected one with a serpentine tip and began probing the lock. "It's a misdemeanor to possess lock picks with intent to feloniously break and enter. However, since I intend to break and enter with permission from the deceased owner's next of kin, we're in kind of a gray area here."

John looked nervously over his shoulder. "I don't think cops recognize gray areas."

"For God's sake, do you see any cops?" I selected a more straight-tipped pick and resumed probing.

"Where'd you get those?" John asked.

"An informant of mine made them for me . . . he even etched my initials on the finger holds. Wiley 'the Pick' Pulaski. He's currently doing four to six for burglary."

"My little sister, consorting with known criminals."

"Well, Wiley wasn't exactly known when I was consorting with him. Good informants can't keep a high profile, you know." I turned the lock with a quick flick of my wrist. It yielded, and I removed the pick and opened the door. "After you, big brother."

The companionway opened into the main cabin—a compactly arranged space with a galley along the right bulkhead and a seating area along the left. I began a systematic search of the lockers but came up with nothing interesting. When I turned, I found John sitting at the navigator's station, studying the instruments.

"Big help you are," I told him. "Get up . . . you're blocking the door to the rear cabin."

He stood, and I squeezed around him and went inside.

The rear cabin had none of the teak and brass accoutrements of the main; in fact, it was mostly unfinished. The portholes were masked with heavy fabric, and the distinctive trapped odor of marijuana was enough to give me a contact high. I hadn't experienced its like since the dope-saturated 'Seventies in Berkeley.

John, who cultivated a small crop in his backyard, smelled it, too. "So that's what pays the mortgage!"

"Uhn-huh." My eyes were becoming accustomed to the gloom, but not fast enough. "You see a flashlight any place?"

He went away and came back with one. I flicked it on and shined it around. The cabin was tidy, the smell merely a residue of the marijuana that had been there, but crumbled bits of glass littered the floor. I handed John the flashlight, pulled an envelope from my bag, and scraped some of the waste matter into it. Then I moved forward, scrutinizing every surface. Toward the rear, under the sharp cant of the bulkhead, I found a dusting of white powder. After I tasted it, I scraped it into a second envelope.

"Coke, too?" John asked.

"You got it."

"Mari and Bryce aren't going to like this. They thought he'd kicked his habit."

"He wasn't just feeding a habit here, John. Or dealing on a small scale. He was distributing, bringing it in on this boat in a major way."

"Yeah." He fell silent, staring grimly at the littered floor. "So what're you going to do . . . call the cops?"

"They'll have to know eventually, but not yet. The dealing in itself isn't important any more . . . its bearing on Troy's murder is."

Back on Point Loma, I waited just out of sight of Troy Winslip's house in the Scout. John had wanted to come along and help me stake the place out, so, in order to otherwise occupy him, I'd sent him off on what I considered a time-consuming errand. The afternoon waned. Behind me, the sky's blue deepened and the lowering sun grew brighter gold in contrast. Tall palms bordering the Winslip property cast long easterly shadows. At around six, a white Dodge van rounded the corner and pulled into Troy's driveway. A young woman—red-haired, willowy, clad in jeans and a black-and-white African print cape—jumped out and hurried into the house. By the time I got to the front door, she was already returning, arms full of clothing on hangers. She started when she saw me.

I had my identification and the release from Troy's parents ready. As I explained what I was after, the woman barely glanced at them. "All I want is my things," she said. "After I get them out of here, I don't care what the hell you do."

I followed her, picking up a purple silk tunic that had slipped from its hanger. "Please come inside. We'll talk. You lived with Troy . . . don't you care why he was killed?"

She laughed bitterly, tossed the armload of clothing into the back of the van, and took the tunic from my outstretched hand. "I care. But I also care about myself. I don't want to be hanging around here any longer than necessary."

"You feel you're in danger?"

"I'd be a fool if I didn't." She pushed around me and hurried up the walk. "Those people don't mess around, you know."

I followed her. "What people?"

She rushed through the door, skidding on the polished marble of the foyer. A few suitcases and cartons were lined up at the foot of a curving staircase. "You want to talk?" the woman said. "We'll talk, but you'll have to help me with this stuff."

I nodded, picked up the nearest box, and followed her back to the van. "I know that Troy was dealing."

"Dealing?" She snorted. "He was supplying half the county. He and Daniel were taking the boat down to Baja three, four nights a week."

"Who's Daniel?"

"Daniel Pope, Troy's partner." She took the box from my hands, shoved it into the back of the van, and started up the walk.

"Where can I find him?"

"His legit business is a surf shop on Coronado . . . Danny P's."

"And the people who don't mess around . . . who are they?"

We were back in the foyer now. She thrust two suitcases at me. "Oh, no, you're not getting me involved in *that*."

"Look . . . what's your name?"

"I don't have to tell you." She hefted the last carton, took a final look around, and tossed her hair defiantly. "I'm out of here."

Once again, we were off at a trot toward the van. "You may be out of here," I said, "but you're still afraid. Let me help you."

She stowed the carton, took the suitcases from me, and shook her head. "Nobody can help me. It's only a matter of time. I know too much."

"Then share it. . . ."

"No!" She slammed the van's side door, slipped quickly into the driver's seat, and locked the door behind her. For a moment, she sat with head bowed, her hands on the wheel, then she relented and rolled down the window a few turns. "Why don't you talk to Daniel? If he's not at the surf shop, he'll be at home . . . he's the only Pope on C Street in Coronado. Ask him. . . ." She hesitated, looking around as if someone could hear her. "Ask him about Renny D."

"Ronny D?"

"No, Renny, with an E. It's short for Reynaldo." Quickly she cranked up the window and started the van. I stepped back in time to keep from getting my toes squashed.

The woman had left the front door of the house open and the keys in the lock. For a moment, I considered searching the place, then concluded it was more important to talk to Daniel Pope. I went back up the walk, closed the door, turned the deadbolt, and pocketed the keys for future use.

Daniel Pope wasn't at his surf shop, and he wasn't at his home on C Street. But John was waiting two houses down, perched on his cycle in the shade of a jacaranda tree.

I raised my eyes to the heavens and whispered to the Lord: "Please, not again!"

The Lord, who in recent years had been refusing to listen to my pleas, failed to eradicate my brother's presence.

I parked the Scout behind the cycle. John sauntered back and leaned on the open window beside me. "Daniel Pope owns a half interest in the *Windsong*," he said out of the corner of his mouth, eyes casing the house like an experienced thief.

I'd assigned him to check into the yawl's registry, but I hadn't expected him to come up with anything this quickly.

John went on: "He and Troy bought the boat two years ago for ninety thousand dollars cash from the yacht broker at Glorietta Bay. They took her out three or four times a week for about eight hours a stretch. In between, they partied. Men would come and go, carrying luggage. Some of the more conservative . . . read that 'bigoted' . . . slip holders complained that they were throwing 'fag parties'."

"But we know they were holding sales meetings."

"Right."

"Where'd you get all that?"

"The yacht broker. I pretended I was interested in buying the *Windsong*. He's probably got the commission spent already. Shit, I feel really guilty about it."

A blue Mercedes was approaching. It went past us,

slowed, and turned into the driveway of the white Italianate house we'd been watching. I unbuckled my seat belt and said: "Ease your guilt by telling yourself that, if you ever do buy a boat, you'll use that broker."

He ignored me, straightening and watching the car pull into an attached garage. "Daniel Pope?"

"Probably."

"So now what do we do?"

Thoughtfully, I looked him over. My brother is a former bar brawler and can be intimidating to those who don't know him for the pussycat he is. And at the moment, he was in exceptionally good shape.

"We," I said, "are going in there and talk with Pope about somebody called Renny D."

Daniel Pope was suffering from a bad case of nerves. His bony, angular body twitched, and a severe tic marred his ruggedly handsome features. When we'd first come to the door, he'd tried to shut it in our faces; now that he was reasonably assured that we weren't going to kill him, he wanted a drink. John and I sat on the edge of a leather sofa in a living room filled with sophisticated sound equipment while he poured three fingers of single malt Scotch. Then I began questioning him.

"Who's Renny D?"

"Where'd you get that name?"

"Who is he?"

"I don't have to talk about. . . ."

"Look, Pope, we know all about the *Windsong* and

your trips to Baja. And about the dealers who come to the yawl in between. The rear cabin is littered with grass and coke . . . I can have the police there in. . . ."

"Jesus! I thought you were working for Troy's parents."

"I am, but Troy's dead, and they're more interested in finding out who killed him than in covering up your illegal activities."

"Oh, Jesus." He took a big drink of whiskey.

I repeated: "Who's Renny D?"

Silence.

"I'm not going to ask again." I moved my hand toward a phone on the table beside me. John grinned evilly at Pope.

"Don't! Don't do that! Christ, I. . . . Renny Dominguez is the other big distributor around here. He didn't want Troy and me cutting into his territory."

"And?"

"That's it."

"No, it's not." I moved my hand again. John did a fair imitation of a villain's leer. Maybe, I thought, he should have taken up acting.

"OK, all right, it's not. I'll tell you, just leave the phone alone. At first, Troy and I tried to work something out with Renny D. Split the territory, co-operate, you know. He wasn't having any of that. Things've been getting pretty intense over the last few months . . . there was a fire at my store . . . somebody shot at Troy in front of his house . . . we both had phone threats."

"And then?"

200

"All of a sudden, Renny D decides he wants to make nice with us. So we meet him at this bar where he hangs out in National City, and he proposed we work together, kick the business into really high gear. But now it's Troy who isn't having any of that."

"Why not?"

"Because Troy's convinced himself that Renny D is small-time and kind of stupid. He thinks we should kick *our* business into high gear and take over Renny's turf. I took him aside, tried to tell him that what he saw as small-time stupidity was only a matter of different styles. I mean, just because Renny D doesn't wear Reeboks or computerize his customer list doesn't mean he's an idiot. I tried to tell Troy that those people were dangerous, that you at least had to try to humor them. But did Troy listen? No way. He went back to the table and made Renny look bad in front of his *compadres,* and that's bad shit, man."

"So then what happened?"

"More threats. Another drive-by. And that only made Troy more convinced that Renny and his pals were stupid, because they couldn't pick him off at twenty feet. Well, this kind of stuff goes on until it's getting ridiculous, and finally Renny issues a challenge . . . the two of them'll meet down in TJ near the bullring and settle it one-on-one, like honorable men."

"And Troy fell for that?"

"Sure. Like I said, he'd convinced himself Renny D was stupid, so he had me set it up with Renny's number two man, Jimmy. It was supposed to be just the two of us, and only Renny and Troy would fight."

"You didn't try to talk him out of it?"

"All the way down there, I did. But Troy . . . stubborn should've been his middle name."

"And what happened when you got there?"

"It was just the four of us, like Jimmy said. But what he didn't say was that he and Renny would have knives. The two of them moved damn' fast, and, before I knew what was happening, they'd stabbed Troy."

"What did you do?"

Pope looked away. Went to get himself another three fingers of Scotch.

"What did you do, Daniel?"

"I froze. And then I ran. Left Troy's damned car there, ran off, and spent half the night wandering, the other half hiding behind an auto body shop near the port of entry. The next morning, I walked back over the border like any innocent tourist."

"And now you think Renny and his friends'll come after you."

"I was a witness. It's only a matter of time."

That was what Troy's girlfriend had said, too. "Are you willing to tell your story to the police?"

Silence.

"Daniel?"

He ran his tongue over dry lips. After a moment, he said: "Shit, what've I got to lose? Look at me." He held out a shaky hand. "I'm a wreck, and it's all Troy's fault. He had fair warning of what was gonna go down. When I think of the way he ignored it, I want to kill him all over again."

"What fair warning?"

"Some message Renny D left on his answering machine. Troy thought it was funny. He said it was so melodramatic, it proved Renny was brain-damaged."

"Did he tell you what the message was?"

Daniel Pope shook his head. "He was gonna play it for me when we got back from TJ. He said you had to hear it to believe it."

The message was in a weird Spanish-accented falsetto, accompanied by cackling laughter: "Knives at midnight, Winslip. Knives at midnight."

I popped the tape from Troy's answering machine and turned to John. "Why the hell would he go down to TJ after hearing that? Did he think Renny D was joking?"

"Maybe. Or maybe he took along his own knife, but Renny and Jimmy were quicker. Remember, he thought they were stupid." He shook his head. "Troy was a dumb middle-class kid who got in over his head and let his own high opinion of himself warp his judgment. But he still sure as hell didn't deserve to die in a parking lot of seventeen stab wounds."

"No, he didn't." I turned the tape over in my hands. "Why do you suppose Renny D left the message? You'd think he'd have wanted the element of surprise on his side."

John shrugged. "To throw Troy off balance, make

him nervous? Some twisted code of drug dealers' honor? Who knows?"

"This tape isn't the best of evidence, you know. There's no proof that it was Renny D who called."

"Isn't there?" He motioned at another machine that looked like a small video display terminal.

"What's that?"

"A little piece of new technology that allows you to see what number an incoming call was dialed from. It has a memory, keeps a record." He pressed a button, and a listing of numbers, dates, and times appeared. After scrolling through it, he pointed to one with a 295 prefix. "That matches the time and date stamp on the answering machine tape."

I lifted the receiver and dialed the number. A machine picked up on the third ring. "This is Renny D. Speak."

I hung up. "Now we've got proof."

"So do we go see Gary Viner?"

"Not just yet. First, I think we'd better report to Mari and Bryce, ask them if they really want all of this to come out."

"I talked with them earlier . . . they were going to make the funeral arrangements and then have dinner with relatives. Maybe we shouldn't intrude."

"Probably not. Besides, there's something I want to do first."

"What?"

"Get a good look at this Renny D."

• • •

An old friend named Luis Abrego frequented the Tradewinds tavern in National City, halfway between San Diego and the border. The first time I'd gone there two years before, John had insisted on accompanying me for protection; tonight he insisted again. I didn't protest, since I knew he and Luis were fond of each other.

Fortunately business was slow when we got there; only half a dozen Hispanic patrons stopped talking and stared when they saw two Anglos walk in. Luis hunched in his usual place at the end of the bar, nursing a beer and watching a basketball game on the fuzzy TV screen. When I spoke his name, he whirled, jumped off his stool, and took both my hands in his. His dark eyes danced with pleasure.

"Amiga," he said, "it's been much too long."

"Yes, it has, *amigo.*"

Luis released me and shook John's hand. He was looking well. His mustache swooped bandit-fashion, and his hair hung free and shiny to his shoulders. From the nearly black shade of his skin, I could tell he'd been working steadily on construction sites these days. Late at night, however, Luis plied a very different and increasingly dangerous trade. "Helping my people get where they need to go," was how he described those activities.

We sat down in a booth, and I explained about Renny D and Troy Winslip's murder. Luis nodded gravely. "The young man was a fool to underestimate Dominguez," he said. "I don't know him personally, but I've seen him, and I hear he's one evil *hombre*."

"Do you know where he hangs out down here?"

"A bar two blocks over, called the Gato Gordo. You're not planning on going up against him, *amiga?*"

"No, nothing like that. I just want to get a look at him. Obviously I can't go there alone. Will you take me?"

Luis frowned down into his beer. "Why do you feel you have to do this?"

"I like to know who I'm up against. Besides, this is going to be a difficult case to prove . . . maybe seeing Renny D in the flesh will inspire me to keep at it."

He looked up at my face, studied it for a moment, then nodded. "OK, I'll do it. But he"—he pointed at John—"waits for us here."

John said: "No way."

"Yes," Luis told him firmly. "Here you're OK . . . everybody knows you're my friend. But there, a big Anglo like you, we'd be asking for trouble. On the other hand, me and the *chiquita,* here, we'll make a damn' handsome couple."

Reynaldo Dominguez was tall and thin, with razor-sharp features that spoke of *indio* blood. There were tattoos of serpents on his arms and knife scars on his face, and part of one index finger was missing. He sat at a corner table in the Gato Gordo bar, surrounded by admirers. He leaned back indolently in his chair and laughed and joked and told stories. When Luis and I sat down nearby with our drinks, he glanced contemptuously at us, then he focused on Luis's face and evidently saw something there that warned him off. There was not a lot that Luis Abrego hadn't come up against in his life, and there was nothing and no one he feared. Renny D, I decided, was a good judge of character.

Luis leaned toward me, taking my hand as a lover would and speaking softly. "He is telling them how he single-handedly destroyed the Anglo opposition. He is laughing about the look on Winslip's face when he died, and at the way the other man ran. He is bragging about the cleverness of meeting them in TJ, where he has bribed the authorities and will never be charged with a crime." He paused, listened some more. "He is telling them how he will enjoy stalking and destroying the other man and Winslip's woman . . . bit by bit, before he finally puts the knife in."

I started to turn to look at Dominguez.

"Don't." Luis tightened his grip on my hand.

I looked anyway. My eyes met Renny D's. His were black, flat, emotionless . . . devoid of humanity. He stared at me, thin lip curling.

Luis's fingernails bit into my flesh. "OK, you've had your look at him. Drink up, and we'll go."

I could feel those soulless eyes on my back. I tried to finish my drink, but hatred for the creature behind me welled up and threatened to make me choke. Troy Winslip had in many respects been a useless person, but he'd also been young and naïve and hadn't deserved to die. Nor did Daniel Pope or Troy's woman deserve to live, and perhaps die, in terror.

Luis said softly: "Now he is bragging again. He is telling them he is above the law. No one can touch him, he says. Renny D is invincible."

"Maybe not."

"Let's go now, *amiga*."

As we stood, I looked at Dominguez once more. This time, when our eyes met, a shadow passed over his. *What was that about?* I wondered. *Not suspicion. Not fear. What?*

Of course—Renny D was puzzled. Puzzled because I didn't shy away from his stare. Puzzled and somewhat uneasy.

Well, good.

I said to Luis: "We'll see who is invincible."

I'd expected the Winslips to pose an obstacle to bringing Renny D to justice, but they proved to be made of very strong stuff. The important thing, they said, was not to cover up their son's misdeeds but to ensure that a vicious murderer didn't go free to repeat his crime. So, with their blessing, I took my evidence downtown to Gary Viner.

And Gary told me what I'd been fearing all along. "We don't have a case."

"Gary, there's the tape. Dominguez as good as told Winslip he was going to stab him. There's the record of where the call originated. There's the eyewitness testimony of Daniel Pope. . . ."

"There's the fact that the actual crime occurred on Mexican soil. And that Dominguez has the police down there in his hip pocket. No case, McCone."

"So what're we going to do . . . sit back and wait till he kills Pope and Winslip's woman, or somebody else?"

"We'll keep an eye on Dominguez. That's all I can promise you. Otherwise, my hands're tied."

"Maybe *your* hands are tied."

"What's that supposed to mean? What're you going to do? Don't give me any trouble, McCone . . . please."

"Don't worry. I'm going to go off and think about this, that's all. When I do give you something, I guarantee it won't be trouble."

When I'm upset or need to concentrate, I often head for water, so I drove north to Torrey Pines State Beach and walked by the surf for an hour. Something was nagging at the back of my mind, but I couldn't bring it forward. Something I'd read or heard somewhere. Something. . . .

Knives at midnight, Winslip. Knives at midnight.

Renny D's high-pitched, cackling voice on the answering machine tape kept playing and replaying for me.

After a while, I decided to do some research and drove to Adams Avenue to find a used bookshop with a large legal section.

CRIMES AGAINST THE PERSON: HOMICIDE. EXPRESS AND IMPLIED MALICE . . . BURDEN OF PROVING MITIGATION— no.

SECOND DEGREE . . . PENALTY FOR PERSON PREVIOUSLY CONVICTED—no.

MANSLAUGHTER COMMITTED DURING OPERATION OF A VESSEL—certainly not.

DEATH OF VICTIM WITHIN THREE YEARS AND A DAY—forget it.

What the hell was I combing the penal code for, anyway?

Mayhem? Hardly. Kidnapping? No, Troy went willingly, even eagerly. Conspiracy? Maybe. No, the situation's too vague. Nothing there for me.

Knives at midnight, Winslip. Knives at midnight.

Can't get it out of my head. Keep trying to connect it with something. Melodramatic words, as Troy told Pope. A little old-fashioned, as if Dominguez was challenging him to a. . . .

That's it!

Duels. Duels and challenges. Penal code, 225.

DEFINED: COMBAT WITH DEADLY WEAPONS, FOUGHT BETWEEN TWO OR MORE PERSONS, BY PREVIOUS AGREEMENT. . . .

PUNISHMENT WHEN DEATH ENSUES: STATE PRISON FOR TWO, THREE, OR FOUR YEARS.

Not much, but better than nothing.

I remember reading this before, one time when I was browsing through statutes that have been on the books for a long time. It's as enforceable today as it was then in 1872. Especially section 231; that's the part I really like.

Gotcha, Renny D.

"I'll read it to you again," I said to Gary Viner. He was leaning toward me across his desk, trying to absorb the impact of the dry, formal text from 1872.

" 'Dueling beyond State. Every person who leaves this State with intent to evade any provisions of this chapter, and to commit any act out of this State, which would be punishable to such provisions if committed within this State, is punishable in the same manner as he would have been *in case such act had been committed within this State.*' "

"And there you have it." I closed the heavy tome with an emphatic *thump*.

Gary nodded. "And there we have it."

I began ticking off items on my fingers. "A taped challenge to a duel at knifepoint. A probable voice-print match with the suspect. A record of where the call was made from. An eyewitness who, in order to save his own sorry hide, will swear that it actually was a duel. And, finally, a death that resulted from it. Renny D goes away for two, three, or four years in state prison."

"It's not much time. I'm not sure the DA'll think it's worth the trouble of prosecuting him."

"I remember the DA from high school. He'll be happy with anything that'll get a slime-ball off the streets for a while. Besides, maybe we'll get lucky and somebody'll challenge Renny D to a duel in prison."

Gary nodded thoughtfully. "I remember our DA from high school, too. Successfully prosecuting a high-profile case like this would provide the kind of limelight he likes . . . and it's an election year."

By the time my return flight to San Francisco left on Saturday, the DA had embraced the 1872 statute on duels and challenges with a missionary-like zeal and planned to take the Winslip case to the grand jury. Daniel Pope would be on hand to give convincing testimony about traveling to Tijuana primed for hand-to-hand combat with Dominguez and his cohort. Renny D was as yet unsuspecting but would soon be behind bars.

And at a Friday-night dinner party, the other half of the "detecting duo" had regaled the San Diego branch of the McCone family with his highly colored version of our exploits.

I accepted a cup of coffee from the flight attendant and settled back in the seat with my beat-up copy of STAN-DARD CALIFORNIA CODES. I had a more current one on the shelf in my office, but somehow I couldn't bring myself to part with this one. Besides, I needed something to read on the hour-and-a-half flight.

DISGUISED FIREARMS OR OTHER DEADLY WEAPONS. Interesting.

LIPSTICK CASE KNIFE. Oh, them deadly dames, as they used to say.

SHOBI-ZUE: A STAFF, CRUTCH, STICK, ROD, OR POLE WITH A KNIFE ENCLOSED. Well, if I ever break a leg. . . .

WRITING PEN KNIFE. That's a good one. Proves the pen can be mightier than the sword.

But wait now, here's one that's *really* fascinating. . . .

The Indian Witch

From the Santa Carla, California *Observer*
January 1, 1900

We called her the Indian Witch, even though her name was really Mrs. Morrissey. Her husband, Thad Morrissey, ran the only saloon in town, and they lived, just the two of them, in a big clapboard house on Second Avenue a few doors down from Main Street. In 1884 Santa Carla was a small town where everybody knew everybody else's business, but no one knew the Morrisseys'.

No one even knew where they had come from. They arrived in town in the fall of 1863: a big, fair-haired, red-faced Irishman and his small, dark Indian wife. Within the week Thad Morrissey bought the saloon and they moved from their rooming house to Second Avenue. Every day at exactly quarter to noon he would walk to the saloon, open up, and spend the hours between then and midnight pouring drinks for loggers who had come into town from the heavily forested ridge that separates Santa Carla from the rugged northern California coastline. He was a genial host, always willing to listen to a man's troubles or extend credit, but he spoke little of himself.

Mrs. Morrissey was even more of a puzzle. From the day she and her husband moved into the house on Second Avenue she never once left it. It was thought

213

she feared shunning from the townswomen, as marriages between whites and Indians were generally viewed as repugnant, but that did not explain why she dared not venture so far as her own yard or deep front porch. A servant girl from one of the town's poorer families did her shopping and presumably was paid well enough that she was reluctant to talk about what she saw and heard inside the big, shadowy house. And so the Morrisseys lived for over twenty years.

In 1882 my family moved to the end of Second Avenue, where grassland spread to the eastern hills. Often my younger brothers and I would play with our friends in the vacant lot across from the Morrissey house. We boys would see Thad Morrissey leave for the saloon and the servant girl come and go, but we never set eyes upon Mrs. Morrissey until one hot July day in 1884, when a curtain moved in an upstairs window and a stern, dark face looked down at us. I was close to the house at the time, having run into the street to retrieve a ball my brother had thrown, and, when I looked up, her gaze met mine.

I shall never forget her eyes: black and implacable—although I would not have known what such a word meant at age twelve—with a flatness that bespoke knowledge of many terrible things. They frightened me so badly that I dropped the ball and fled back to the safety of the lot. And on that day we christened Mrs. Morrissey the Indian Witch.

Every day for the rest of July and August we would wait for her to appear in the window. Every day she obliged us on the stroke of three. She would remain there, unmoving, watching us at play for exactly ten minutes. When school began in September, she would watch us as we walked home. By then it seemed to me that I was the object of her gaze.

September passed quickly, and then it was October: lemon-yellow days with a chill on the evening air. But shortly before Halloween, as if nature were angry at the passage of summer, heat enveloped our inland valley. On the coast the dog-hole ports, where logging companies sent their timber down chutes to schooners at anchor in the coves, were unnavigable because of fog, but Santa Carla experienced no such relief. And on one of those still, blazing afternoons Thad Morrissey toppled forward as he reached across his bar to pour whisky for a logger and died at the age of sixty-two.

Word of his death spread quickly through town. We boys gathered at the vacant lot after school to see what would transpire at the Morrissey house. A delegation of men, including Doc Bolton and Mayor Drew, arrived. They were met by the servant girl, who spoke briefly with them. The next day we learned the Indian Witch had sent instructions through her that her husband was to be buried without ceremony in a plot he had purchased in the graveyard. The townsfolk were shocked to hear it was a single plot. Thad Morrissey had made no provision for his wife, and not even a funeral wreath adorned the forbidding house's door. The Indian Witch continued to appear at the upstairs window, but now she seemed to study me more intensely.

The heat wave finally broke, and November turned chilly. Our thoughts moved forward to Thanksgiving and Christmas. One evening nearly three weeks after Thad Morrissey's passing I was walking by his widow's house on the way to visit a friend when a voice spoke to me.

"Young man, come here!"

I stopped, my blood suddenly colder than the air, and peered into the shadows. She was on the porch, wrapped in a black shawl, her hand beckoning to me. My first impulse was to run, but curiosity overcame it and I moved closer.

"Come up on the porch, please."

The voice was refined with scarcely a trace of an accent, not at all as I had imagined it. Or perhaps I had not imagined her as possessing any sort of voice, so stony and silent had she seemed as she stood at the window. I ascended the steps slowly.

The Indian Witch looked me up and down, taking my measure. Then she nodded as if satisfied with what she saw. "I want you to do something for me," she said.

"Ma'am?" The word came out a croak.

She brought out her other hand from beneath the shawl and extended a folded sheet of paper. "I have here a list of things to be purchased. I will reward you for doing so."

"But your girl. . . ."

"Martha cannot perform these errands. No one is to know these things are for me. Will you do this?"

I looked into her eyes and saw both pride and pleading. Then I nodded and held out my hand for the paper, which was thick with money tucked into its fold.

"Why did you choose me?" I asked.

"I have watched you. I know you are trustworthy. Bring the things tomorrow night." Then she turned and went into the house.

I forgot about my visit to my friend and ran home, clutching the Indian Witch's list. My brothers were in the bedroom we three shared and my parents in the parlor, so I took the list to the kitchen, where a kerosene lamp burned low, and examined it.

The items puzzled me: a pair of sturdy boots in the smallest available size, heavy socks, a warm jacket, a small pack, dried meat, and other portable foodstuffs. It appeared to me as if she were about to embark upon a long hike, except in those days respectable matrons of our town did not walk great distances (and, so far as I know, still do not).

I saved my errands for late the next afternoon, as I was sure they would attract notice and I wanted my father to return from his work at the grain mill before anyone could question him about his son's unusual purchases. By the time he heard about them, the deed would be done, and I would have quite a story to tell. My father loved nothing more than a good story.

By suppertime my shopping was completed and the

bundles, along with some extra money, stowed behind our outhouse. I could barely taste my food for my excitement. As soon as I could, I slipped out, retrieved the bundles, and carried them to the Indian Witch's house. She was waiting on the porch, wearing the same black shawl, but on this night she beckoned me inside.

To my surprise, the house was quite ordinary, not much different from my own. She motioned for me to deposit the bundles beside the front door, then bent to look through them. When she straightened, she had the extra money in her hand.

"Yes, I was right about your trustworthiness," she said. "I always could judge a good man."

A good *man*. My heart swelled at the compliment.

She handed me the money. "I want you to have this."

My reward! I had thought perhaps a piece of pie or cake. But this was too much money, five dollars.

"I cannot accept. . . ."

"You can and you will. Come into the parlor, please."

I followed, clutching the money, wondering what else she had in store for me.

A fire burned on the hearth, strong and steady. She had laid and lighted it herself, which impressed me, as my father always proclaimed women incapable of such acts. The Indian Witch motioned me toward a large chair that must have been Thad Morrissey's, and claimed a cushioned rocker for herself. She gripped its arms with long-fingered hands, and, when she looked into my eyes, the firelight made hers glitter fiercely.

She said: "I know what you call me, you and your friends. 'The Indian Witch'."

I gulped and could say nothing.

"It is because I am different. You need to put a name to that difference, so you imagine I have evil powers."

"Ma'am. . . ."

"Be quiet! I have decided to tell you my story. Perhaps it will teach you not to judge others until you know the reasons behind their differences. But first you must promise to tell no one."

"I. . . ."

"Promise!"

I promised. And then she began.

My story begins in the winter of Eighteen Fifty-Six. My tribe . . . I am Pomo . . . had always lived on Cape Perdido, at the northwestern boundary of this county. The rains were bad for two years, the sea worse. Fish and game were scarce, the wild plants even more so. My father could not feed our family.

There was a man who ran a saloon in the logging town on the ridge who was known to be charitable. My father went to ask his help, taking me along. My father was proud. He did not want to beg, and the man knew that. So he bargained. He would give food in exchange for me, Wonena. I was fourteen years of age, the man thirty-four. His name was Thaddeus Morrissey.

My father had no choice but to agree to this proposition. The family would have starved otherwise. For myself, I was not afraid to stay. As I said before, I could always judge a good man. A lesser man than Thaddeus Morrissey would have made me his slave and turned me out when he tired of me. But instead he married me and gave me my Christian name, Emma. He moved me into his rooms above the saloon, asked a neighbor woman to teach me to cook and bake bread and keep house. In the mornings, before he went downstairs, my husband taught me English. He laughed at my mistakes, but gently. He in turn learned words and phrases from my language. In time I came to love him, and he to love me. I think perhaps he had loved me from the first, although we never spoke of it. I became more white than Indian.

In Eighteen Sixty-One we began to hear rumors. A white man had discovered oil on my tribe's land on Cape Perdido. Now the big companies wanted to drill wells there, but the tribal council said they would never permit it. Those lands were their hunting and gathering grounds. Their ancestors' spirits dwelled there. Cape Perdido was sacred to them.

The government, of course, was on the side of the big companies. They sent troops to force the Pomos off their land. This, of course, was happening to Indians everywhere when valuable things were found on their lands, and some fought back. My tribe decided to fight back, also.

Do you know Perdido means something not easily

tamed? In those days it was even more rugged and wild than now. The Pomos knew that cape, but the government soldiers did not. For over a year they stumbled into the ravines and got lost in the forests and fell from the steep cliffs, while the Pomos hid in natural shelters and moved invisibly across the land, killing the intruders one by one.

Finally the government agreed to peace talks with the Pomo leaders. They were three . . . my uncle, my cousin, and my brother. I remembered my uncle and cousin as violent men, my brother as easily led by them.

The Army officers had heard of me, Emma Morrissey, who used to be Wonena. They knew I could speak both English and my own language, and that these leaders were my people. The officers conscripted me to accompany them to the talks.

My husband was against my going. He feared my tribesmen would harm me, or the officers abandon me should trouble arise. But the officers were insistent, and I wanted to help bring about peace. As I said before, I had become more white than Indian.

At dawn on the day of the talks my husband and I met the officers at a stage stop at the foot of the ridge. They also were three . . . General Shelby, Commander Bramwell, Indian Agent Avery. My husband cautioned them to protect me. He said he would wait at the stage stop for no more than four hours, and then follow us. General Shelby said we would return long before then.

We set out for the meeting place, an ancient clearing

in the forest that was sacred to the tribe. There, three boulders stood in a row, as if cast down by the heavens, as no rocks similar to them existed for miles. I rode astride my horse, trying to remember the faces of my brother, uncle, and cousin, but it had been too many years since I had parted from them. All I could see was stone. Three great stones, hiding three stone faces. And with that vision, the knowledge of what was to happen grew upon me.

I reined in my horse, called for the others to halt. I told them that, if they went to the clearing, they would surely be killed. They scoffed at the notion, refused to believe me. The Pomos had given their word to the government, the general said. They would not dare break it. I pleaded with the men, told them of my vision. I wept. Nothing I could do or say would stay them. We rode on.

When we arrived, the clearing was empty. The boulders stood before us . . . massive, gray, misshapen. All around us redwood trees towered, the sun shining through their misted branches. Nothing moved or breathed. The clearing no longer felt sacred, because death waited behind those boulders.

General Shelby was angry. "These savages have no timepieces," he complained. He dismounted, began pacing about.

It was then I saw the barrel of the rifle move from behind the boulder nearest us. It was then I shouted.

The shot boomed, and a bullet pierced General Shelby's chest. Blood stained his uniform.

As the general fell, Commander Bramwell wheeled his horse and galloped from the clearing. He was abandoning me, as my husband had feared the soldiers would.

Indian Agent Avery was confused. A second bullet from behind a second boulder brought him down before he could take shelter or flee.

From behind the third boulder my brother, Kientok, stepped. He aimed his rifle at me, but he did not fire. After a moment he lowered it and said in our language: "Another day, Wonena." Then all three were gone into the forest.

Weak and weeping, I made my way back to the stage stop where my husband waited. When I told him what had happened, his lips went white, but he said nothing, simply took the reins of my horse and led me home. By the next afternoon he had sold the saloon and loaded all our belongings into our wagon. We journeyed inland, and, when we moved into this house, I found that I could not leave it. If my whereabouts were discovered, soldiers would come for me. Surely Commander Bramwell would want to destroy an Indian woman who could brand him a coward. Men from my tribe might come to exact retribution. I believed that so long as I remained indoors with my loaded pistol at hand I would be safe. But I was not safe from the fear. It became my constant companion. It ate at our lives, as did my husband's knowledge of what I would surely do after his passing.

Shortly after my husband and I came to Santa Carla,

my tribe was defeated. My uncle and cousin, upon the testimony of Commander Bramwell, were hanged for the murders of General Shelby and Indian Agent Avery. My brother and a number of other men escaped to the ridge, but most of the tribe was removed by the government to a reserve in Oregon. The oil companies drilled their wells on Cape Perdido. Like the wells at Petrolia in Humboldt County, they soon went dry. Oilville, the town that had grown around them, fell into ruins.

Few of the Pomos returned to their lands after they were abandoned by the white man. The Oregon reserve had become home to them. My brother and his renegade band dwell on the cape, however, and now, my duty to my husband fulfilled, I must return to them and take up the threads of my life. My husband knew I would do so, and this is why he made no provision for my burial at Santa Carla.

This, young man, is the story of Emma Morrissey. Now the story of Wonena will begin.

After I left Emma Morrissey's house that November night, I waited, cold and cramped, behind a manzanita bush in the vacant lot. I was aware that by now my parents had discovered my absence and would punish me upon my return, but it seemed small price to pay to view the conclusion of Mrs. Morrissey's story.

I was rewarded when, at half past midnight, a small, shadowy figure emerged from the house and moved down the porch steps. It wore a warm jacket and sturdy boots and carried a small pack that I knew to be filled with provisions for a long journey. Emma Morrissey did not look back at the place that had been her prison for the past twenty years, but merely slipped down the street and disappeared into the darkness as invisibly as her tribesmen had moved across Cape Perdido over two decades before.

I remained where I was, shivering and wondering if Mrs. Morrissey believed the lies she had told me. Her self-imposed confinement to the house had not been out of fear, but in penance for betraying her own people. And she was not making her journey to Cape Perdido to take up the threads of her former life. Instead, this woman who had become more white than Indian would return to face the retribution that her brother, Kientok, had promised with his final words to her: "Another day, Wonena."

The boy to whom Emma Morrissey told her story is, of course, I, Phineas Garry, editor of this newspaper. You know me as a serious, middle-aged man of many words and opinions, most of which have inflamed the more conservative elements of our population. For nearly a decade, outraged readers have asked me why I espouse certain causes, particularly those I support of the rights of our natives.

I have chosen the dawning of this new century to break my long-kept promise and tell the tale that has shaped my life, in order that Wonena should not have lived—and died—in vain.

The Cyaniders

Historians claim that we were the people who broke the wild spirit of the American gold mining frontier, and I suppose in a way it's true. We came west armed not with picks and shovels but with university degrees in engineering; we rode into the moribund camps and towns not on mules or horses but in hired coaches. And we staged a quiet revolution that changed the mining world forever.

I changed my particular part of that world—the Knob mineral district in Soledad County, California—more than most of my colleagues. I, you see, was the lone woman among the four men who came there.

The Knob is exactly what its name implies: a bald, rounded outcropping rising above thick piney slopes, which in the 1860s was host to one of the richest veins of gold in the northwestern part of the state. But when I first came there, it stood as a monument to played-out mines, waste dumps, and near-deserted towns. Its desolation cast a pall over the verdant forest and cañons that then, in autumn, were choked with golden-leafed aspen. Its shadow darkened the nearby town of Seven Wells, giving its few remaining citizens pause about spending another hard winter there.

None of that mattered to me, not then. As I stood looking up at the Knob, far from the mountains of my native Colorado, I saw not the rotting timbers of the mine adits and sluices, but the richness of the autumn foliage and the festiveness of the red berries that hung in abundance on the thorny pyracantha shrubs. Where others saw ruin, I saw opportunity for rejuvenation. The tailings that spilled down the hillside to a nearby creek were a blight, of course, as was the mill, which had not been stripped of its equipment, but soon the Knob would once more bustle with activity. I took great breaths of the crisp air and knew that I'd come to a special place that would own a part of me forever.

It was the tailings and the remaining poor-quality veins of ore that had brought the five of us to Soledad County. Some dozen years before, in the late 1880s, three Scotsmen had developed a method by which cyanide was used to leech gold from such unlikely sources. In 1889 the Forrest-MacArthur process was first used on a production basis at the Crown Mine at Karangahake, New Zealand, and now, in 1900, various United States metallurgical teams had reported varying degrees of success with it. The proprietors of the firm for which I worked, Denver Precious Metals, were men who detested being bested by their competitors; they had quickly acquired title to most of the defunct mines in the Knob district and dispatched their cyaniders, as we came to be known, on an exploratory mission.

I speak with authority about Matthew and Peter Lazarus, co-owners of Denver Precious Metals. They were, respectively, my father and my uncle. Both a love of mining and an unflinching desire to be the biggest and the best runs thickly in the veins of all our family members.

The town of Seven Wells, so named for its abundant underground springs, lay in a narrow meadow between Soledad County's thickly forested coastal ridgeline, where logging was king, and the rugged, sparsely inhabited foothills of the Eel River Forest. It once numbered nearly ten thousand in population, and housed two hotels, two general stores, various shops, twelve boarding houses, fifteen saloons, and seventeen brothels. Of these, only the general store, a few shops, and a hotel-and-saloon of dubious repute remained. Small homes fanned out from the town center, but most were abandoned and deteriorating; as we drove along the main street, I saw the same was the case with those buildings that lined it. A few old men sat on benches in front of the store, and three children played ball in the park-like grounds surrounding the stone-walled public well across from it, but foot traffic on the sidewalks was light.

It had been decided that during our initial stay in Wells I was to board at the home of one Widow Collins; I was delivered there while my colleagues went on to settle into their quarters at the hotel. My father and mother had indulged me in many ways, but they stood firm on the issue of my residing in an establishment that was a former brothel, with four mining engineers who, in my father's words, were no better than they should be. So up onto the front porch of the Widow Collins's neat little house I went, carrying a full load of rather dire preconceptions. Fortunately they were all disproved by the pretty, plump woman who greeted me, with a small boy peering out from behind her blue skirts.

Dora Collins was only a few years older than I, twenty-eight at most. Her brown eyes were warm and lively, her cheeks flushed with excitement at the prospect of a visitor. Her dark hair was in rebellion, exuberant curls escaping from the bun at the nape of her neck. She took my grip and ushered me inside her home, setting the bag down and clasping both my hands in hers.

"Miss Lazarus," she said, "you have no idea how honored I am to make your acquaintance."

"Please call me Elizabeth."

"If you'll call me Dora. And this"—she nodded at the boy, who was now peering from around a door-jamb—"is Noah."

Noah's response to the introduction was to scamper away.

"He's shy," his mother said, "but in no time he'll take to you. Now, let me show you to your room, and then we'll have a cup of tea. I'm ever so anxious to hear about the business that brings you to Seven Wells."

It was the beginning of a firm friendship.

Dora Collins, I learned in the course of our conversation over tea and scones, had been born and raised in the logging town of Talbot's Mills, some thirty miles to the southwest. She had married her childhood sweetheart, a manager with Seven Wells Mining, and moved there with him in 1890. Three years later, when they were beginning to despair of having a child, the boy, Noah, was born. And the year after that William Collins was killed in a freak accident at the mine site.

"Why did you stay on?" I asked her.

"I thought I could do some good here. You see, the mine had been operating at minimal capacity ever since we arrived, the town shrinking year by year. But there were still children who needed educating, and before my marriage I had trained to be a schoolteacher. For the past five years I've been conducting classes in my parlor, but now I have only three pupils. Their families will soon be leaving, and so will Noah and I."

"To go where?"

"Back to my family in Talbot's Mills." Her eyes clouded. "I don't really wish to do that. We haven't been on good terms since my marriage, but a woman in my position has no other choice. But enough about me. How did you come to be an engineer?"

It was a question I was often asked, so I had a ready response. "My father claims mining is in the family blood. Since I am an only child, it was my duty to carry on the tradition. My mother is herself an educated woman, and felt her daughter should enjoy the same advantages. I attended Colorado School of Mines with their blessing, and, after thoroughly reviewing my academic record, my father hired me."

"You must have visited so many interesting places and seen so many wonderful things."

"Actually this is the first time I've set foot outside Colorado."

"And you've never . . . ?" She hesitated. "Forgive me if I ask too personal a question."

"Please, ask freely." I knew what her question was.

"You've never married?"

"No. There was someone, and we had planned. . . . But he was killed in an accident similar to your husband's."

Her eyes moistened with understanding, and she touched my arm. "I am so sorry."

"It's a long time past," I replied, although the day four years ago that my fiancé had died still seemed like yesterday. "And I have my work, as you have your son."

The next morning I met with the others at the former assay office on Main Street that was to be our headquarters in town. As we unpacked the record-keeping supplies and laboratory equipment that would enable us to test the strengths of the sodium-cyanide solutions and later the quality of the gold it would precipitate, the men told me about their evening.

"The saloonkeeper at the hotel says there's a good bit of resentment over us coming to town," Adams Horton said. Hort, as he was known, had worked for Denver Precious Metals from the beginning. The big, ruddy-faced, white-haired man was as much of an uncle to me as Peter Lazarus, and he had promised my parents to look out for me during our stay in California.

"Because we've bought up title to most of the mines?" I asked.

"And because we're able to extract the gold with relative ease, while the few remaining miners must struggle for theirs. We are outsiders, and the townspeople are afraid we'll leave the town poorer."

"Poorer!" Tod Schuyler snorted. "After the sum we parted with in that saloon last night?"

Tod was in his thirties, married, but said to have an eye for the ladies. Indeed, he was handsome, but his overly friendly manner and lack of seriousness, to say nothing of his heavy indulgence in drink, did not endear him to me.

John Estes, a childless widower with a thin, angular frame and sparse gray hair, spoke. "You know what Hort means, Tod. Seven Wells is a dying community. Everyone, from the shopkeepers to the miners with small claims, is bound to resent us." John was a senior engineer at the company and knew the mining culture well. He was also a kind man who had helped me refine many of the techniques I had learned at the School of Mines.

"What was the name of that Cornishman?" Uncle Hort, as I called him, asked.

John Estes paused to think. "Trevelyan. Andrew Trevelyan. He and his brothers came over from Cornwall in 'Forty-Nine. Did well in the Mother Lode . . .

the Cornish are talented miners. Then they came here, staked their claim, but it was a poor one, nothing like the others near the Knob. Trevelyan is old now, and bitter. Angry, too. The saloonkeeper says he's made threats."

"Against us?" I asked.

"Among others."

"Are you worried about them?"

"No." He shook his head. "As I said, Trevelyan's old, and an idle talker. There's nothing to be afraid of."

I glanced at the fifth member of our team, Lionel Eliot. He was my age, and had joined the company only three months before. A bachelor, he had revealed little of himself on our journey to Seven Wells. Now his lightly freckled face—a suitable companion to his thick reddish hair—was thoughtful. His pale blue eyes met my gaze levelly, and, in the few seconds before he looked away, I saw they were deeply disturbed.

"What do you know of a man called Andrew Trevelyan?" I asked Dora. It was late in the afternoon, and we were having tea.

"Trevelyan? What makes you ask?"

"My colleagues have heard that he's made threats against us."

Dora compressed her lips, frowning. "I would have caution, then. He's a brutish man."

"But old."

"And still dangerous. He beat his wife for years,

233

until one of their grown sons took her off to live with his family in Sacramento. And there is a rumor that he killed his own brother in a dispute over their mining claim."

"Killed him? How?"

"No one knows. The brother, Conrad, disappeared. No trace of him has ever been found. And a week later the other brother, Wesley, left town and never returned. They say Wesley witnessed the murder and was afraid for his own life."

"But this is only rumor."

"Rumor has a way of attaching itself to the proper object. When you see Andrew Trevelyan, you will understand what I mean."

I had that dubious privilege three days later, after returning to the assay office after spending a morning at the Knob supervising the unloading of steel drums of cyanide from I.G. Farben and milling equipment from the Krupp Works. Dora had arrived, bringing me a surprise meal of bread and cheese and hard-cooked eggs, and, after we had finished, she suddenly drew me to the window fronting on Main Street. Motioning to a man striding along the opposite sidewalk, she said: "Andrew Trevelyan."

He was brutish-looking and, while old, showed no signs of weakness. Well over six feet, he towered above the people he passed, his barrel chest thrust out, big fists pumping the air as if to punish it. His hair was a wild grayish-white tangle, his thick-featured face coarsely textured and wrinkled. His clothing—flannel shirt, leather vest, denim trousers—looked none too clean even at a distance, and his heavy boots were caked in mud. Both women and men gave him wide berth as he strode along, casting what I assumed were evil looks at all he encountered.

"I now understand what you meant by rumor attaching itself to the proper object," I said to Dora.

"And why I told you to have caution."

"I wish the men were here so we could point him out to them."

"He will point himself out to them before very long, I assure you."

The next week passed quietly and productively. We collected our samples from the tailings and waste dumps, and adjusted our cyanide solutions to achieve maximum recovery of the gold. Dora had asked me if I were not discomforted by working with such a deadly poison, and I had explained that in its diluted state it was quite benign. Gold, and silver, too, had an affinity for cyanide and would attach itself to it; later we would run the resultant solution through zinc shavings, which would precipitate the precious metal. The Forrest-MacArthur process was a simple one, and rendered safe because cyanide was neither unstable nor corrosive, or explosive.

In the quiet of the former assay office Lionel Eliot and I performed our tests and recorded our results, while the others supervised the setting up of the mill at the Knob and hiring of miners to extract the low-grade ore that remained in the earth. During those hours we spent together, Lionel and I seldom spoke, but it was not an uncomfortable silence. In fact, after a day spent conducting tests, I emerged as refreshed as if it had been devoted not to work but to sleep. And that was fortunate because, as Dora had predicted, young Noah had taken to me with the energetic zeal of a seven-year-old, constantly entreating me to join in his games and read him stories. Dora was disconcerted and cautioned him to leave me be, but Noah had found a willing playmate in "Auntie Elizabeth". It had been four years since I felt such simple joy, and now I began to delight in the rhythm of my days.

That rhythm was broken at the beginning of our third week in Seven Wells. It was late afternoon, and, feeling a stiffness in my back, I had risen from my chair and gone to the window overlooking Main Street. A figure on the far sidewalk drew my attention: Andrew Trevelyan leaning against the wall of the abandoned building behind him, his large arms folded across his chest, a peaked cap pulled low on his brow. Distance and shadow could not disguise the malice on his coarse-featured face as he stared at me. Quickly I stepped back from the window and said: "Mister Eliot?"

Lionel Eliot looked up from the logbook in which he was recording the results of a test we had completed earlier on a sample of low-grade ore. Before he could speak, I motioned for him to join me. When he saw

Trevelyan, his breath escaped in a hiss.

"Do you think we have something to fear from him?" I asked.

He hesitated, then shook his head. "No. I've been talking with people about Trevelyan . . . the shop-keepers, the men who sit in front of the general store. To a man, they fear Trevelyan, but they say he seldom engages in confrontation unless provoked. Still. . . ."

"Yes?"

"I would rather you did not walk back to your lodgings alone today. If I may, I'll escort you.

"I would be pleased." Very much, in fact. During the hours we had spent in one another's presence, I had come to like and respect Lionel Eliot. Although he was a quiet and non-assuming man, I sensed a deep and rich vein of strength ran through his core.

Andrew Trevelyan was across the street the next day, and the next. Lionel Eliot escorted me both to and from our office, and one of the other men was always with me when my presence was required at the Knob. The mill was nearly ready to operate, and initial tests of the equipment were being made.

On the afternoon of the third day of Trevelyan's presence, Uncle Hort returned from the Knob earlier than usual for the purpose of having a talk with Trevelyan. Lionel Eliot and I watched as he crossed the street and approached the big Cornishman. After a few moments of discussion, Uncle Hort turned and came back to the office.

"Mister Trevelyan," he said, "claims he has taken a fancy to that particular spot because the sun shines upon it in a manner that pleases him."

"The sun!" I exclaimed. "That side of the street is mainly in shade."

Uncle Hort nodded. "He also claims that he bears us no ill will. 'If I'd gotten myself an education like you people, I'd be more than a dirt-poor miner,' he told me. 'You people were smart to look to the future.'"

"Was he sincere?" I asked.

He snorted. "Sincere? Lizzie, you may be a grown-up lady with an engineer's degree, but sometimes I question your good sense."

I felt the blood rush to my face and could find no suitable response.

Lionel Eliot, however, surprised me. "On the contrary, Hort," he said, "I think Miss Lazarus has excellent instincts. There may be more to this Cornishman than any of us realizes."

Uncle Hort erupted with laughter. "If you discover his good side, you must be certain to inform me of it. And what is this 'Miss Lazarus' nonsense? Formality isn't necessary among us. She's Lizzie to John, Tod, and me, and should be Lizzie to you as well." With that embarrassing pronouncement, he moved to the back of the room where he began pawing through the test logs.

Lionel Eliot smiled sympathetically at me. "Do you like to be called Lizzie?"

"Not really. It makes me sound twelve years old."

"Then may I call you Elizabeth?"

"You may. But what shall I call you?"

"Not Ly, as the others do. It makes me sound untruthful. I prefer Lionel. It means lion-like."

"Lionel," I said. The name suited him perfectly.

Three days later, days in which Andrew Trevelyan kept his vigil in the sunless patch on the opposite side of Main Street, Lionel and I entered the office in the morning to find the others already assembled. Uncle Hort and John Estes looked grave. Tod Schuyler seemed subdued, and he had a dark, knotted bruise on his high cheek bone. His eyes were reddened, his complexion pale. Too much whiskey the night before, I supposed.

Before I could ask what the trouble was, Uncle Hort said: "There has been a confrontation with the Cornishman, Lizzie. I will spare you the more sordid details"—this with a meaningful glance at Tod Schuyler—"but I feel that from now on a man should stay under the roof with you and Missus Collins. On our way to the Knob, we will stop there and ask if John may rent a room from her."

"This confrontation. . . ."

"Ly will tell you about it. We must go now."

I watched as they filed out, noting that Tod walked stiffly, cradling one arm to his ribs. "Lionel," I said, "exactly what are these 'sordid details'?"

He smiled. "Hort said that would be the first thing you would ask. And, unlike him, I feel you are woman enough to hear them. Yesterday evening Tod was drinking in the hotel saloon with a woman whose reputation is not above reproach. The kind of woman who. . . ."

"I know what kind of woman frequents saloons, Lionel."

"Of course. Her name is Addie Lawton, and she is a good deal older than Tod. Her husband deserted her a number of years ago, and since then she's made her living by. . . ." Lionel looked so discomforted that I had to smile.

"I am not easily shocked," I told him. "And I am aware of what goes on when a woman is left penniless and a man like Tod is far from home. Please continue with your story."

As the hours went by, Lionel said, the whiskey flowed. Tod and his companion became loudly intoxicated, so they scarcely noticed when Andrew Trevelyan strode into the saloon. The Cornishman went directly to their table and pulled Tod from his chair, shouting that no sissified mining engineer from Denver was going to steal his woman. As he began to drag Tod toward the door, Addie Lawton followed, urging Tod to stand up to Trevelyan. But Tod went limp in Trevelyan's grasp, and, when they reached the street, the Cornishman hit him on the face. After he fell to the ground, Trevelyan kicked him several times in the ribs."

"And then?" I asked when Lionel paused.

"Then Addie Lawton called Tod a coward and left with Trevelyan."

I did not care for Tod Schuyler, but I regretted that he had been humiliated in such a fashion. Men like Lionel or John or Uncle Hort could tolerate such insult, but it must have dealt a crushing blow to Tod.

As if he knew what I was thinking, Lionel said: "Yes. I'm afraid that Schuyler may have difficulty showing his face on the streets after this incident. Hort has offered to allow him to return home."

"But he's essential to the team."

"No one is that essential."

Tod Schuyler remained in Seven Wells, but as a changed man. He no longer frequented the saloon, and spent many hours brooding in his room. Gone was his jocular and overly familiar manner. He performed his work silently, his mouth set in grim lines. Often he absented himself from town and the mill for hours, riding about the countryside. And he did not join in at the gatherings that occurred several times a week at Dora's house, now that John was boarding there. Dora and Noah had taken to John much as they had to me. When he asked if he might invite Lionel and Uncle Hort to supper one night, Dora readily agreed. Other suppers followed.

Andrew Trevelyan had withdrawn from our lives as well, and it was a relief not to find him staring from across the street every time I looked out the office window. The townspeople said that, since the night he beat Tod, he had stayed close to his cabin on Drinkwater Creek, and the woman, Addie Lawton, stayed with him.

As autumn turned to winter and Thanksgiving approached, my days resumed their pleasant rhythm. Operations had begun at the mill, and Uncle Hort began to speak of returning to Denver for Christmas. John and Lionel said they would prefer to remain in Seven Wells. As for myself, I welcomed the opportunity to spend my first California Christmas in Dora Collins's cozy home, with the people who I was beginning to regard as family.

Then, the day before Thanksgiving, all the windows in our office were smashed. No one had seen or would admit to having seen the culprit, who had struck sometime after Uncle Hort had left there at six in the evening. We had the windows boarded over, and got on with our work as best we could, but all of us, even the usually unshakeable John Estes, were nervous and irritable. Tod Schuyler became even more withdrawn, and Lionel said that he had taken to drinking alone in his room. The incident cast a shadow over the Thanksgiving feast Dora and I prepared, and shortly after that Uncle Hort cancelled his plans to spend Christmas with his grown children in Denver.

Finally, the next Monday, John Estes was shot.

It happened in the morning at the Knob. A shot rang out in a thick copse of trees along the creek, and a bullet struck him in the shoulder, its force knocking him back into a waste dump. No one saw the shooter, although later Tod Schuyler discovered some broken branches that showed where he must have stood.

Quickly two workers loaded John into a wagon and brought him to Dora's house, unconscious and bleeding profusely. Uncle Hort arrived behind them on horseback and spoke grimly of transporting him to a doctor.

Dora said: "The nearest doctor is thirty miles away, over bad roads. A journey of that sort could kill him. Bring him inside."

"Bring him inside to die?" Uncle Hort exclaimed.

Her eyes flashed both annoyance and amusement. "I can doctor him as well as anyone. In the mining camps, we women quickly learn such skills."

A chastened Uncle Hort motioned for the workers to carry John inside.

Dora asked my assistance, and we went upstairs to John's room. The wound, she found, was not as serious as the profuse bleeding had led her to believe, and the bullet had not lodged there. While she cleaned and bandaged it, we heard Lionel arrive, and then Uncle Hort's voice rose from the parlor, loud and strident.

"We know the identity of our shooter, Ly. It is that Cornishman. A coward, hiding in the trees with his rifle! Tomorrow morning I am riding to Talbot's Mills to inform the deputy sheriff there about these incidents."

Lionel said something in a low voice.

"You're right that we have no concrete proof of his involvement, but circumstances support it," Uncle Hort replied. "The man killed his own brother. . . ."

"Again, there's no proof."

"Nevertheless, I am determined to talk with the sheriff without further delay."

While Lionel and I walked to our office the next morning, he informed me that Uncle Hort had left for Talbot's Mills at first light. After we were seated at our desks, he grew silent, and, although he made a show of paging through his logbooks and notes, I sensed he was troubled. By noon, when I decided to return to Dora's house to see how John was mending, he still hadn't spoken and paid me little attention as I gathered my things and went out the door.

I found Dora in the kitchen making a soup stock. John was resting comfortably, she told me. "He is all for getting out of bed and going after the Cornishman himself," she added. "I fear that John will not be an easy patient."

I noted her use of John's first name; up to now she had referred to him as Mr. Estes. "How long will he be bedridden?" I asked.

"As long as I can persuade him to remain there. Perhaps a day."

"I've never known him to be troublesome."

She smiled mysteriously. "Men are always troublesome when they seek to impress. . . ."

A knock came at the kitchen door, and a woman's voice called out Dora's name. There was a frantic quality to it that made my friend raise her eyebrows in alarm. Quickly she set aside her wooden spoon, and went to see who was there.

It was Millicent Wilson, a neighbor whose son Tommy frequently played with Noah. Her eyes were round and frightened, her face pale. She grasped Dora's arm, exclaiming: "You must come!"

Dora reached for her cloak where it hung on a peg inside the door. "What is it?"

"My Tommy and your Noah. They're very ill."

I followed the two women outside as Dora asked: "How ill? In what way?"

"They're dizzy and breathing with difficulty. Noah's limbs are twitching."

Now Dora paled. "When did these symptoms start?"

"They were playing near the well in the park across from the general store when I did my marketing. Tommy says they both drank of it and immediately became sick. This was perhaps fifteen minutes ago."

Dora hurried toward Millicent's small white house. "I'll need warm soapy water to begin. And afterward, salt water, also warm. Wood ashes from your stove and vinegar will also help."

Recognizing the course of treatment she planned to follow, I asked in a low voice: "Poison?"

She nodded grimly. "I'll force them to regurgitate the stomach contents, and then neutralize what remains. In the meantime, I need you to go to the general store and ask them to close off the well."

"Of course." But before it was closed, I would take a sample of the water.

"Cyanide," I said, looking up from the laboratory table at Lionel. "We are fortunate that the well water diluted it so much. Otherwise, we would have had two dead boys."

His face was deeply troubled. "We should also take samples at the other public wells and close them until we can make an analysis."

"And then we should inventory our supplies of cyanide at the mill."

The six other public wells in town were tainted, and an entire drum of cyanide was missing from our stores. While Lionel rode about warning the owners of private wells about possible contamination, I looked in on Noah and Tommy and found that Dora's doctoring had been successful. Thanks to her quick assessment of their symptoms, their discomfort had been shortened.

By the time I returned to our office, a crowd was gathering—an angry crowd demanding we take our poison and return to Denver. I urged them to remain calm, assured them the trouble was well in hand, but they only became louder and more enraged, so I locked the office door and withdrew to the rear, wishing for a steadying presence. But Uncle Hort was in Talbot's Mills by now; John was in his invalid's bed at Dora's house; Tod was at the mill; and Lionel was probably taking samples at the private wells. The job of defending the office and reputation of Denver Precious Metals had fallen to me, and I felt a poor champion at best.

• • •

After perhaps an hour, the noise outside, which had fallen off to a murmur, again rose to a din. Above the townspeople's voices I heard that of Tod Schuyler. I went to the front of the office and pressed my ear to the still boarded window, trying to hear what he was saying.

"Yes, it was our cyanide!" he shouted. "But if you want to place the blame, look to the Cornishman, Andrew Trevelyan. He's held a grudge against Denver Precious Metals since we arrived here, and I caught him skulking around the shed where the cyanide drums are stored on the night one of them disappeared."

The crowd's noise grew louder, an ugly, ominous growl that made the skin on my arms prickle.

"The Cornishman has no regard for human life," Tod went on. "Ours, yours, or your children's."

He spoke on in that vein, inciting the crowd. Perhaps the Cornishman deserved retribution, I thought, but not at the hands of an angry mob. And what of his woman, Addie Lawton? She could also become their victim.

I knew what I must do. After fetching my cloak, I slipped out the rear door of the office into the alleyway and hurried to the stable where we kept our horses.

Drinkwater Creek had been a mere trickle when we arrived in early autumn, but recent rains had swelled it to a fast-moving stream. I followed its banks some five miles from town through thick woods, my horse stepping gingerly over rocks and tree roots, until I came to a lightning-split eucalyptus that Lionel had once told me marked the boundary of the Cornishman's claim. Then I turned east, away from the creek, toward a plume of wood smoke that drifted above the pines. Emerging from the trees, I found a clearing where a rough board shack stood. As I approached, a woman stepped out, a rifle cradled in her arms. Her hair was disheveled, her long skirts dirty and torn, her face bore deep lines that told of long exposure to the harsh elements.

"Addie Lawton?" I asked.

"I am. And you are that woman from the mining company."

Of course, in a town as small as Seven Wells she would know who I was. "Elizabeth Lazarus," I told her. "May I speak to you?"

"If you must."

"And Mister Trevelyan, if he is at home."

Her lips twisted mirthlessly. "He is at home, yes. But can you speak to him? I think not."

"This is a matter of life or death."

Again, the strange humorless smile. "Then come in."

Addie Lawton and I were waiting outside the cabin when the mob arrived, Tod in the lead. He drew his horse to a halt when he saw us, rifles in our arms. The others followed suit.

"So," he said, "the coward sends out women to defend him. What are you doing here, Lizzie? This is no affair of yours."

"It is my affair when unjust accusations are flung about."

"Then you should be with us, and against them." He motioned at Addie Lawton, then the cabin. To her, he added: "Go inside and send out the Cornishman."

She stared at him, her eyes hard.

I said: "I'm afraid she can't do that."

"Why? He's here, isn't he?"

"He is, in a fashion."

The crowd was silent now, listening closely. Tod glanced back at them. "You speak in riddles, Lizzie."

"Very well, I'll speak plainly. Andrew Trevelyan died this morning. Of pneumonia. He became ill two weeks ago and has been bedridden ever since. It's quite impossible that he smashed our office windows, shot John Estes, stole our cyanide, or poisoned those wells."

Tod's face reddened. "Did she"—again motioning at Addie Lawton—"tell you that?"

"I saw his body with my own eyes. He could not have done those things. But an enemy of his could. An enemy who had access to our office . . . and to the cyanide at the Knob. And who claims he saw Andrew Trevelyan 'skulking' around the mill the night the cyanide was taken. Yet the same person was unsure earlier today as to when the drum disappeared."

The men with Tod were beginning to cast suspicious

glances at him. He saw their expressions and, without another word, whirled his horse and galloped off into the woods. A murmur of unrest traveled through the crowd. One man shouted: "He's the one she's talking about!"

Fearing the mob would now turn its rage upon Tod, I said: "Leave him be. Mister Horton has gone into Talbot's Mills for the sheriff's deputy."

"But he'll escape before the deputy arrives!" another man cried.

"Mister Schuyler won't go far. Men like him are unaccustomed to fleeing on horseback, particularly in a snowstorm."

A few flakes had touched my cheeks in the past minute. The men in the crowd turned their faces to the sky and watched the snow begin to fall more thickly. Then, in silence, they turned their horses toward town.

Tod Schuyler was apprehended while struggling through the high drifts near Talbot's Mills the next morning, after being thrown by his horse and spending the frigid night in an abandoned cabin. Although there was no substantial proof of my allegations against him and formal charges were never brought, his career with Denver Precious Metals was over. Early in the new year, he abandoned his family and disappeared into Mexico.

The poison in the wells diluted quickly, and, with the spring run-off, they were pure once more. The memory of the incident so remained in the consciousness of Soledad County's populace, however, that they took to calling Seven Wells Cyanide Wells. Several years later, it became the official appellation.

The Forrest-MacArthur process proved very successful for us, and eventually earned great profit for the company. In April, John Estes was appointed mill manager at the Knob. He and his wife, the former Dora Collins, and their son Noah still live in Cyanide Wells.

Uncle Hort went back to Denver, but within a year he was off to Montana's copper country. A restless man with an insatiable appetite for new places, he nevertheless stays in contact with those he holds dear.

In July of that fortuitous New Year, Lionel and I boarded a stage for Virginia City, Nevada and the Comstock Lode. There we became known as the first husband-and-wife cyaniders—a title that might sound ominous to many, but to us signifies a sharing of the life we love.

Additional Copyright Information

"Sweet Cactus Wine" first appeared in *The Arbor House Treasury of Great Western Stories* (Arbor House, 1982) edited by Bill Pronzini and Martin H. Greenberg. Copyright © 1982 by the Pronzini-Muller Family Trust.

"The Sanchez Sacraments" first appeared in *The Ethnic Detectives* (Dodd, Mead, 1985) edited by Bill Pronzini and Martin H. Greenberg. Copyright © 1985 by the Pronzini-Muller Family Trust.

"Cave of Ice" first appeared in *Boys' Life* (6/86). Copyright © 1986 by the Pronzini-Muller Family Trust.

"Time of the Wolves" first appeared in *Westeryear* (M. Evans, 1988) edited by Edward J. Gorman. Copyright © 1988 by the Pronzini-Muller Family Trust.

"Sisters" first appeared in *New Frontiers 1* (Tor, 1990) edited by Bill Pronzini and Martin H. Greenberg. Copyright © 1989 by the Pronzini-Muller Family Trust.

"The Lost Coast" first appeared in *Deadly Allies II* (Doubleday, 1994) edited by Robert J. Randisi and Susan Dunlap. Copyright © 1994 by the Pronzini-Muller Family Trust.

Center Point Publishing

600 Brooks Road ● PO Box 1
Thorndike ME 04986-0001 USA

(207) 568-3717

US & Canada:
1 800 929-9108